Devlin's anger and frustration rose beyond his self-control. He wanted to hit something, had to hit something. He began to overturn desks and chairs. He picked up a chair and threw it across the room. It landed on the teacher's desk, knocking off a cup and saucer, which smashed into pieces on the floor.

Dog Tucker

K. DRINKWATER

SCHOLASTIC
AUCKLAND SYDNEY NEW YORK LONDON TORONTO
MEXICO CITY NEW DELHI HONG KONG

First published in 2009. This rejacketed edition
published in 2021 by Scholastic New Zealand Limited
Private Bag 94407, Botany, Auckland 2163, New Zealand

Scholastic Australia Pty Limited
PO Box 579, Gosford, NSW 2250, Australia

ISBN 978-1-77543-723-9

National Library of New Zealand Cataloguing-in-Publication Data

---

Drinkwater, K. (Kathryn)
Dog tucker / K. Drinkwater.
ISBN 978-1-869-43893-7
[1. Problem youth—Fiction. 2. Teenage boys—Fiction. 3. Uncles—Fiction. 4. Responsibility—Fiction.] I. Title.
NZ823.3—dc 22

---

12 11 10 9 8 7 6 5 4 3 2 1 1 2 3 4 5 6 7 / 2

Publishing team: Lynette Evans, Penny Scown and Abby Haverkamp
Cover design by Smartwork Creative, www.smartworkcreative.co.nz
Cover photos: iStock.com / bigstockphoto.com
Typeset in Berthold Imago 11/16.5pt by Book Design Ltd
Printed and bound in Australia by Griffin Press, part of Ovato

Dedicated to the memory of my fourth form
(Year Ten) English teacher, Mr R.W. McCullum,
who encouraged me by calling me
"The writer"

CHAPTER ONE

Devlin tried to ignore the whispered taunts coming from behind him. He sat at his school desk with his head down, but he had given up pretending he could understand the words on the page. His olive complexion paled, as his thick brown hair – too long at the front – fell over his dark eyes.

"Devlin-wevlin, foster-boy imposter-boy."

A pudgy boy called Jimmy repeatedly whispered the sneer. Other boys sitting close by snorted and sniggered. Some copied him.

At the front of the room Mrs Mackay continued writing year-nine English homework on the board, unaware of the tension building at the back of the classroom.

Devlin reached breaking point. He swung around in his chair and shouted, "Shut up! Just shut up, you loser!"

"You're the loser, devil-boy," Jimmy answered in a low, menacing voice.

Mrs Mackay turned around just in time to see Devlin slam his fist into Jimmy's face.

"Fight, Jimmy! Fight! Fight!" The other boys shouted encouragement as the two became locked in a wrestle.

Blood from Jimmy's nose splattered over both of them. The boys grunted as fists flew and chairs overturned.

"Stop it, boys! What do you think you're doing?" Mrs Mackay rushed towards them. Her protests were drowned out by the bell. School was finished for the day.

Jimmy slipped out of Devlin's grip, grabbed his bag and took off. The other boys followed, eager to catch up with him and gloat over their victory.

As the classroom emptied, Devlin found himself left facing the glaring teacher.

"Devlin Hunter! Principal's office, first thing in the morning!" she barked.

Devlin's anger and frustration rose beyond his self-control. All of his past, the hurts, the disappointments, boiled into this moment. He wanted to hit something, *had* to hit something. He began to overturn desks and chairs. He picked up a chair and threw it across the room. It landed on the teacher's desk, knocking off a cup and saucer, which smashed into pieces on the floor.

He stopped, suddenly shocked and appalled. Mrs Mackay was trembling, mouth open. Devlin felt sick.

The classroom door opened. A slender lady with blonde hair held back in a ponytail, peeked in. Seeing the chaos, her eyebrows lifted and she stepped inside.

"Devlin? You weren't waiting for me in the car park so I came looking for you. What's happened?"

"I'm afraid we have another problem, Mrs Kent." Mrs Mackay glanced at Devlin as she spoke in a shaky voice. "A very *big* problem. I'd like you to take Devlin home now - he can tell you what he did. You will need to bring him into the principal's office first thing in the morning."

Devlin watched his foster-aunt's face. He didn't like the disappointment in her eyes, so he looked down at his feet.

She reached under his desk for his schoolbag. He tried to lunge for it saying, "I'll get it, Aunty Rose." He was too late. She picked it up, opened it and became very still. Packets of chips, chocolate, muesli bars of all kinds and even three yoghurts were plain to see.

Both women looked at Devlin with even deeper disappointment.

Mrs Mackay broke the silence. "I see we have found the lunch thief," she said coldly.

"Yes," Rose quietly agreed. She removed the items and placed them on a desk for Mrs Mackay. "We'll see you in the morning, Mrs Mackay, thank you. Come on, Devlin, time to go."

Rose carried his bag for him while Devlin followed. He put on a mask of toughness and his 'don't care' attitude as he sauntered from the classroom and out to the car.

In his mind he was predicting what would happen next; first, a lecture in the car on the way home. Aunty Rose was a kind lady, he'd give her that much, she'd probably try to give him a chance to voice his thoughts and feelings, but in the end, what difference would it make? He would still get a lecture. Then the social worker would have to be called, then would come the dreaded session in the principal's office in the morning.

He'd been through it all before, with other foster families and other schools. He felt like he was on a nightmare ride in a ghost train with no way to get off. So many things were out of his control and he just had to go through it all.

But each upsetting encounter seemed to be building on the last. Each loss of a foster family or a school left him wondering how to cope, while he was still being launched into new ones.

He sat sullenly in the front passenger seat, waiting for Rose to start her lecture. But she seemed to be focusing on driving home through the West Auckland suburb of Massey.

Devlin wondered if he would be sent for another counselling session. He liked his counsellor, but sometimes felt like the hour was just a brief holiday from life. Reality always hit him full force as soon as he walked out the door.

He felt all tense inside. His worst fear was to be sent away, to another home, another school. He thought about running away, before they got the chance to tell him he wasn't good enough, that they didn't want to have to deal with him and his 'behaviour problems'.

"Devlin …" Rose took a deep breath.

Here we go …

"Devlin, why did you steal that food? I give you a good lunch. If you want more, you know you only have to ask. There isn't anything those kids have that you don't have. So why?"

"I don't have a *dad* … or a real home," he mumbled. "That's something they have that I don't. Mum's had her rest from us kids – how come I'm the only one still waiting to go back?"

"So does it make you feel better to steal?"

Devlin shrugged his shoulders, not looking at her.

"You know you do have a home," she reminded him gently. "Your mum's had time out and had her new baby and it will be your turn to go home soon. It's not easy to care for four littlies under five on your own—"

"And cope with a problem kid as well," he finished for her. His eyes betrayed the hurt rejection he felt at this thought.

"I wasn't saying that—"

"You don't have to. My mum told me. The counsellor has told me. The social worker has told me. I have no dad because he never wanted to know me. Everybody tells me I'm a problem – and nobody wants me! I don't belong anywhere." He choked on the last words, emotion getting the better of him.

He could tell Rose felt saddened at his words. He sensed she cared, but she was like him, riding the ghost-train roller coaster and powerless to change his circumstances.

"*I* want you," she said quietly and firmly. "But I also want to see you work through some of these … 'issues' you have." She glanced at him and smiled gently. "We'll face it all … together … okay?"

Devlin didn't answer. He stared down at grubby toes sticking out of his school sandals. He was afraid to accept her offer. Afraid she would let him down. He wanted to trust her, wished that he could, but a self-protective fear kept it locked away inside of him.

"Mr Selleck, won't you even consider it?" Aroha Bentley gazed imploringly at the stern gentleman. They sat opposite each other on comfortable couches in a cheerfully decorated lounge.

The window behind Aroha looked out on horses grazing on this Southhead farm, and beyond to the Kaipara Harbour. The window behind the stocky, grey-haired man showed more of his farm acreage and a stunning view of a lake, surrounded by forest spreading out to meet the New Zealand west coast and Tasman Sea. Some of the farm's trees were changing early to autumn reds and golds, creating eye-catching colour.

"Miss Bentley, I have been on my own for nine years now," he swallowed painfully, and took a deep breath, "and you are asking me to take on a thirteen-year-old boy with behavioural issues – and you want me to home-school him as well! I hardly think I am the right candidate, do you?"

Aroha gazed at him out of soft brown eyes. Her dark

hair was swept back from her tanned face. "In many ways it would be a challenge for you, I agree," she replied, "but in other ways you are a good candidate. You are mature. There are no other children here to divert your attention. You can provide stability. Your references tell me you would be a wonderful male role model. You and your late wife completed your foster-care training."

"That was a long time ago and now she's not here to do it with me."

"You can do a refresher course. You are also the only relative in a position to take him."

"Being the youngest cousin of his grandfather is a pretty distant connection. Surely there must be someone closer? An uncle or aunt?"

Aroha shook her head. "It's my job to look into this sort of thing and believe me, you are the only one I could consider at this time. He is placed with a very loving foster family at present, but now that I have found you, I am obliged to approach you. It is preferred that we place children with relatives, where possible."

George Selleck set his mouth in a hard line. "I'm sorry, Miss Bentley—"

"Please – call me Aroha."

"Aroha … but my answer is no. I'm sure he will be okay with his foster family. They are probably providing a much better form of care than I ever could." He stood. "Shall I walk you to your car?"

George stood in his driveway, watching the social worker drive away down the rutted, loose metal road. Further along, a cloud of dust indicated an approaching vehicle. His face softened as a silver Mercedes appeared in the distance. The two vehicles slowed to pass each other on the long driveway and moments later the Mercedes came to a stop in front of George's house.

"G'day, George!" his friend Allan greeted him cheerily, getting out of the car. He was a tall, solid man, clean-shaven with silver-grey hair, dressed in casual slacks and a smart, woollen jersey. "Did I miss an important visitor?"

"Believe it or not, a social worker came to see me," George spoke in his usual gruff voice.

Allan chuckled. "A social worker? Did she have the right man?"

"Nah, of course not," George answered abruptly.

Allan looked at him shrewdly. "She wanted something you weren't prepared to give, right?"

"Right. She wanted me to give some rascal boy a place to live! Can you imagine it? Me, been on my own so long!"

Allan looked thoughtful as he removed his boots and

headed for the open front door, saying over his shoulder, "Never known you to turn down a challenge. You could do with a helping hand about the place. But you're right, maybe you're getting too old," he chuckled. "Not too old to make me a coffee, I hope." He disappeared inside.

George stood glaring after him.

Devlin lay in the dark on his bed, thinking. The school principal had suspended him, so he hadn't been to school for a week. He was glad. He wished he didn't have to go back at all. *Strange sort of punishment,* he mused, *I got the very thing I wanted – no school! If only I didn't have to go back tomorrow…* The more he thought about it, the more his stomach churned, and he tossed and turned on his bed. Then he became still as an idea formed in his mind. He mulled it over for a long time.

At last he went into action. *No going back,* he told himself. As quietly as possible he emptied his school bag and refilled it with clothes and a pocketknife, a picture of himself with his mum and four younger half-brothers and sisters, a youth Bible Aunty Rose had given him and an ice-cream container holding a small rock collection.

The rock collection was something he had begun the

first time he had to leave his mum. She had pressed a small, brownish pebble into his hand as she said goodbye. "Just because you aren't with me, doesn't mean I don't love you," she'd whispered. "Let this rock remind you of that, okay?"

He nodded, but her words hadn't made the changes any easier to endure. After that, he would pick up a small stone every time he let go of a home. He had collected six stones so far.

One of those stones was from the last stay with his mum, who at that time was heavily pregnant. His sister Tracy and brothers Zachary and Sammy had each, one by one, returned from foster care to live with her again.

Devlin had been visiting for the Christmas holidays. He didn't like to remember that visit. In the past, his mum's boyfriends had physically and verbally abused her and her children. This time was no different.

The boyfriend's name was Greg. Devlin disliked him at first sight and it appeared the feeling was mutual. He pushed Devlin and the smaller children around a lot when Mum wasn't looking. Then, when she entered a room to find one of the kids crying, Greg would lie and say Devlin had caused the problem.

Devlin found it wasn't any use arguing. Greg had well and truly pulled the wool over his mum's eyes.

She would get angry, wrongly thinking Devlin was the cause of the trouble in the house and lose her temper with him. Then she would burst into frustrated tears. Finally, she sought help, the social worker came, and Devlin returned to his foster home.

Devlin bunched up his fists. He hated Greg for robbing him of his home. He hated his mum for not listening. He hated the social worker for not taking him back to his mum after he told her the truth. It was easier to hate everyone, to turn his back on them all. Somehow it made him feel he had some control.

He stood at the window of his small bedroom, staring out into the night. Aunty Rose and Uncle Jack slept in the next room. Further down the hall, in the only other bedroom, their sixteen-year-old daughter, Helena, was also asleep.

They had all been good to him. He couldn't complain about them not trying to make him welcome and help him fit in. But the way things were going he feared it wouldn't be long before they couldn't cope any more and would want to send him away.

Silently he opened the window and climbed out. He stood on the grassy lawn under the windowsill. A new feeling of elation welled up inside him. Freedom! He had no idea where he would go, only that he was in control and nobody could reject him again. This time, he had turned his back on them all.

Still not making a sound he walked across the front lawn. He felt a momentary pang of guilt as he imagined the upset look on Rose's face once she found him gone. For a brief moment he paused to pick up a small stone from the driveway, putting it in his container. Then he hardened his heart and marched along the footpath of the well-lit, suburban street.

Devlin headed for Henderson, following the maze of streets, sometimes flat and sometimes hilly. There was a surprisingly regular amount of traffic passing him, even at one o'clock in the morning. He crossed Lincoln Road and took another road, which he thought headed south.

He jumped nervously as some newspaper rustled in the shadows of a building. Looking closer, he saw the shape of someone curled up, trying to sleep on a bench seat. *Someone homeless*, he thought. Then it struck him: *Like me.*

The early-autumn night air was cool and crisp. His breath came out in large puffs of cloudy vapour. As he trudged, his eyes became heavy with the need to sleep.

Devlin was walking over a bridge when a police car, travelling silently behind him, suddenly turned on its siren. He jumped and swung guiltily towards it but it shot past him, responding to a call. He let out a long breath of relief.

At the end of the bridge, Devlin noticed a path going down to the left. The reflections of streetlights glinted on the silent river below. Thinking he might find somewhere to rest until morning, he began walking down the path.

At the bottom, a noise from under the bridge made him pause and stare into the darkness. Slowly he made out the shapes of several teenagers. One of them was sniffing at something under his jacket. Probably glue. Devlin felt uneasy. This group of street kids may not welcome a stranger. He began to turn to the right, planning to follow the path away from them.

A hard thump on his back sent him sprawling, face down on the concrete. In seconds he had leapt to his feet and spun to face his attacker. He was surrounded by roughly dressed teenagers – a mix of nationalities. He saw the flash of a knife blade and cold fear struck him.

"Give us your money." The one brandishing the knife spoke in a low, threatening tone. He had orange-bleached hair and dark skin. He smelt as if he hadn't washed in weeks.

Devlin struggled to find his voice. "I – I don't have any!" At that moment he regretted wearing the clothes Rose had bought him. They made him look richer than he was.

Devlin wondered if he was about to be knifed and decided he'd rather not wait to find out. Taking his attacker by surprise, Devlin kicked the knife out of his hand. It flew through the air and landed with a plop in the river.

Furious, the group came at him all at once, shouting and swearing. They punched, kicked and shoved him until he hit the ground. Then they kicked him some more. Devlin put his arms around his face and head. He felt a hard blow to the top of his skull and then everything faded into black.

CHAPTER TWO

George awoke with a start, sweating. The strong feelings from his dream were still with him. He had lost count of how many times he had dreamed the same thing. But this time the ending was different. The screams of his wife and ten-year-old son, echoing in his ears, were the same. And his own voice, screaming their names. But this time, at the end, it all blended into a different picture. Suddenly he was watching a lonely-looking teenage boy with his back to him, leaning down over two graves.

George lay in silence for a while. His fast-beating heart returned to normal. He couldn't stop thinking about the boy. Eventually he muttered into the darkness, "Confounded social worker! And damn you, Allan."

He lay thinking until the chill of dawn crept into the bedroom, then he rose, dressed and headed out into the cool, clean air to feed the horses.

A few hour's later, George phoned the social worker.

"What do you mean – you don't know where he is?" George asked Aroha incredulously.

"I was afraid it might come to this, George." Aroha explained. "Sometimes this sort of thing happens and unfortunately, if we can't nip it in the bud, it becomes a habit. The young person can become what I call a 'runner'."

"Where should I start looking for him?" George asked.

"No, George, it's not your job to look for him, you need to leave that in our hands."

George spluttered indignantly but didn't argue.

"I think it's wonderful that you have thought it through and are willing to take him on, though. That's the best news I've had all week. Normally we would try to bring him out for a weekend to introduce you to each other, but under these circumstances, I'm not sure how things will turn out. I'll keep you informed though."

"He'll be all right once he gets here, won't he?" George asked.

"The biggest challenge is whether we can succeed in getting him to settle down. This time, sending him to you may be the last chance for this boy to get himself together. If he becomes a constant runaway, life will become very difficult for everybody, I'm afraid."

After George hung up, he sat with his head in his hands. Doubt plagued him. What on earth was he doing? What was he taking on? Was he crazy to disturb the comfortable, quiet, simple life he was used to?

Later, he voiced these thoughts to Allan, who had called in for one of his frequent visits.

"Just look on it like he's a racehorse, George," said Allan. "What happens when you get given a rogue to sort out?"

George answered, "Usually they're just scared to bits on the inside because they haven't been handled properly."

"So you get their trust, and … in time … you have a bargain on your hands," Allan finished.

George chuckled, blue-grey eyes twinkling. He had huge respect for Allan, his friend of twenty years. "Somehow, Allan, I don't think this boy will be as predictable as a racehorse, and *they're* unpredictable enough."

Allan smiled, a gleam in his eye. "The bigger the

challenge, the bigger the reward, eh mate?" Changing the subject, he said, "I'm off to the races Friday night. You want to come?"

George frowned in mild annoyance. "Allan, you know I haven't been for years. Stop asking me."

Allan ignored the answer. "A few of your old mates have been asking after you. One of the horses you sold a few months ago is running in race three. They've got the top New Zealand driver on it – you know – Saraia Smith. I'll give you a lift and even shout you dinner. It's a pretty decent feed." Then he added, "Besides, there's been a bit of funny business happening there lately. Can't quite put my finger on who it is, but I reckon there's something dodgy going on. Wouldn't mind your opinion on it."

George stubbornly shook his head. "I haven't been since … since I stopped training for myself. You know that. I can't be bothered with it."

Allan knew. He remembered how he and his wife had become friends with George and Helen when the couple first came to Southhead. Helen was pregnant at the time. Ten years later he had supported George through the aftermath of terrible tragedy. And over the last nine years, he had subtly helped George pick up his life again, bit by bit.

"Anyway," George joked, "I thought you were a

Christian man, Allan? What does your church have to say about you going to the races?"

Allan laughed and answered mysteriously, "I'm simply a worker in a field, mate." He put down his empty coffee mug and stood. "Think I'll give Betty a run around the track this morning. You got that two-year-old ready for jog-work yet?"

George gave a puzzled frown but let Allan's vague answer go. Helen had attended Allan's church. That was how they had become friends. George had respected Helen's right to believe in God, but did not agree with her. Since the accident he would wonder sometimes if he would see her and his son again in another place. But following that line of thought led somewhere he wasn't prepared to go. So he would brush the niggling thoughts aside and focus again on here and now.

He shook his head in regard to the two-year-old. "Another week I'd say."

His mind returned to the conversation with Aroha. "What do you think about this boy – Devlin's his name – disappearing like that?"

Allan chuckled. "Hunger will bring him out. Wait and see."

Devlin woke with a groan. His head hurt. Everything hurt. He opened his eyes and found himself staring up at the graffiti on the underside of the bridge. He was alone and his bag was beside him, the contents strewn over the concrete. One of his old T-shirts was hanging off the low bank, dangling in the water. Several ducks quacked as they swam past, watching him warily with their dark eyes.

He sat up slowly. Putting his hand to the top of his head he found the tender lump there that he expected.

An early morning jogger pounded her way down the footpath to the right of him. She glanced at him curiously.

Feeling foolish and self-conscious, Devlin collected his clothes. He guessed the street kids must have searched his bag. The photo and Bible were still in the side pocket and his ice-cream container was upside down on the grass. He found all seven rocks scattered around it. The pocketknife was gone. He repacked his bag and sat watching the ducks, feeling miserable.

After a while his stomach rumbled. *Why didn't I think to raid the pantry before I left?* he wondered. The ducks swam this way and that through the sparkling water. Overhead, cars and trucks roared and rattled across the bridge.

Devlin thought about the good breakfast he was

missing back with his foster family. With a groan he remembered the box of his favourite cereal Rose had bought specially for him.

More early-morning joggers glanced at him curiously, as they ran along the riverside walkway. The sun shone, warming the bank. The grass looked soft and inviting. Ignoring the passersby, he moved out from under the cold shadows of the bridge and lay face down, stretched out on the grass. Enjoying the soothing warmth of the sun, he closed his eyes and dozed.

It was mid-morning when he woke. He sat up, feeling a bit better but even more hungry. Two women walked along the path on the bridge above him, smiling and chatting. Their clothes made him think they were office workers on their morning tea break. He stared hard at one of them, thinking she looked familiar.

Once over the bridge they turned towards him and disappeared behind a wall of greenery. He realised they were taking the path down beside the river, and soon they were in front of him.

The familiar woman's eyes met his.

Devlin leapt up off the grass in shock.

"Devlin Hunter!" Aroha was equally amazed to be staring at her lost charge.

He turned to run.

"Devlin! No – wait! Please! I've got some good news."

Slowly, he turned back, eyeing her suspiciously. Then he noticed the sandwiches in her hand.

She smiled. "Hungry?" She held out the food. Her companion stood back, watching with interest.

"Yeah." He made no move towards her. "I don't want to go back to that school," he said, warily watching her face.

"You don't have to now, Devlin." She gave him a beautiful, beaming smile and said firmly but kindly, "Come on. We've got another option to talk about. Feel like a burger? I'll get you some food and we can talk."

Devlin weighed it up. Freedom and going hungry? Or trusting Aroha and filling his stomach? Curiosity and hunger won the argument and he decided he could always split on her later.

The three quietly walked up the path and over the bridge until they came to a car park. Aroha's friend bid them farewell and disappeared into an office building. Aroha unlocked her car and held open the door for Devlin.

Minutes later they were sitting at a burger bar. While Devlin stuffed his face with a burger and hot chips, Aroha phoned Rose to tell her that Devlin had been found. Then she waited patiently for him to finish eating.

Finally his hunger was satisfied and he felt a lot less grumpy. "Is Mum ready for me to come home?" he asked hopefully.

Aroha's eyes were compassionate. "No, Devlin, not yet. I do want you to know though, that I took what you told me about Greg seriously and we are keeping a close eye on things. I need to make sure your little brothers and sisters are safe."

Devlin felt sick with disappointment. "There's no good news then," he mumbled into his empty burger box.

"Not that kind, anyway," Aroha answered gently. She studied his face. "How'd you get those bruises on your face?"

He shrugged his shoulders, ashamed to tell her.

"You okay?"

He nodded and mumbled a lie, "They're from that fight at school, you know. I guess they just showed up late."

Aroha sighed, protective and indignant. "No wonder you don't want to go back there!"

Devlin nodded, not meeting her eyes.

"I've found a relative who would like you to come and live with him. He's a distant cousin of your mother's father – an older man, in his late forties. He lives by himself on a farm. Lost his wife and son years ago in an accident."

"What's his name? Have I met him before?" Devlin asked curiously.

"George Selleck. He says you can call him Uncle George. No, as far as I know you haven't ever met him before."

"Will I have to go to a new school?"

Aroha smiled. "Nope. Not a public one, anyway. You're a long way behind in your schooling. Mr Selleck – Uncle George – has agreed to supervise you on a home-schooling programme. He says you'll be getting up early and working on the farm until breakfast. After breakfast you'll be doing your schoolwork. After lunch you'll be doing 'practical learning'."

"But I've never lived on a farm before ..." Devlin felt a small spark of excitement, mixed with the usual fear, at this proposed new home.

"I know, but that doesn't matter. George will help you learn all about it."

Another upsetting thought suddenly occurred to Devlin. "What about Aunty Rose? Why am I moving again? Don't they want me back?"

"Aunty Rose definitely *would* like you back. She's disappointed at the idea of you moving, but says she's happy you have a relative to go to and thinks you'll enjoy the farm."

This answer made Devlin feel a little better, but as usual he felt turmoil at the idea of another change.

"I have to be honest with you, Devlin. Uncle George looks like a tough character. I don't think he will take any nonsense. He has a good heart though – he'll be fair."

Devlin swallowed nervously. "When do I go?"

"Well, we could go and say goodbye to Aunty Rose and take you out there today. The quicker we get you settled in your new home and back into your schooling, the better. Okay?" She gave him a reassuring smile.

"I guess I can give it a go," Devlin mumbled, knowing that he'd just take off again if he hated it.

Devlin watched Rose through the car window as Aroha pulled away from the curb. She was smiling in a sad sort of way and waved until the car went out of sight.

He felt the usual tearing sadness deep down; letting go of people he had once dared to hope would be his final foster family, before returning to his mum. But he did the only thing he knew to cope with it. He pushed his feelings down deep, and hardened himself. His outward mask became a little tougher, another layer thicker.

Aroha glanced at him and felt concerned at the shadows in Devlin's eyes, the angry set of his mouth. She hoped this new placement would work out for him.

The drive took them out along State Highway 16, past orchards and wineries. They took a left turn and passed through the small township of Parakai. Devlin noticed a heated swimming pool complex.

"Do you think Uncle George will let me go to the pools?" Devlin asked hopefully.

"I expect so, sometimes. It's important for you to practise water skills. I'll suggest he makes it part of your school programme, if he hasn't already thought of it. Okay?"

"Cool." Devlin hoped he could go to the pools soon.

The road seemed to go on and on. The further they went, the more and more isolated it felt. Aroha concentrated quietly on the windy road.

What if this man, Uncle George, was as mean as some of Mum's boyfriends? Devlin wondered.

Suddenly, the idea of being left, stranded in the middle of nowhere, alone on a farm with a stranger, scared him immensely. He felt more vulnerable than he had facing the street kids last night, and felt himself mentally and physically shutting down. Then, suddenly, he went to sleep.

Aroha observed him with some concern. She knew that sometimes falling asleep suddenly is a sign a foster child isn't coping with the stress of change. She had seen

Devlin do it often enough to know it wasn't a coincidence or just the motion of the car.

He awoke as Aroha drove up a rough road lined with old pines and willow trees. A dozen or so horses stood in large, fenced paddocks. As the car rounded a bend, a modern brick home came into view. A large implement shed and various other large farm buildings sat to the right of it.

"Look at that!" Devlin had seen the breathtaking view of the west coast meeting the Tasman Sea. "This place must be up really high."

"Yes," Aroha agreed, smiling, "and look over the other way – that's the Kaipara Harbour."

Devlin turned his head and saw the distant harbour glinting in the sun.

As they drew up in front of the house, a black and white farm dog leapt off the front steps and bounded towards the car, barking furiously.

Devlin saw a stocky man come out the front door. He was wearing a dark green jersey and brown corduroy trousers. His grey-brown flecked hair was trimmed short and half hidden by an old cap advertising 'Harness Racing'. He appeared rather grim, Devlin thought, as though he didn't smile very often. *What am I in for?*

CHAPTER THREE

George watched the car come to a halt. He saw Aroha get out, but mostly he watched the lanky, bruised, brown-haired boy. The boy's fringe reminded George of a horse's forelock, the way it flopped down over his dark, wary eyes. He felt concern at the bruises on his face. Was it his imagination or did the boy seem slightly stiff and sore, favouring one leg?

As Devlin stood beside the car, George observed the boy's I'm-tough-and-don't-touch-me stance. He could read fear and mistrust in every part of the boy's body language, disguised as aggression. *What am I in for?* he wondered. He made sure his expression didn't give away his thoughts as he walked forward. "Hello, Aroha."

He smiled at her then stepped towards the boy, hand outstretched. "Hello, Devlin."

Devlin shook hands, looking uncomfortable and uncertain. "Hi, um, Uncle George."

George spoke to Aroha, "I'll help carry his bags."

"This is all my stuff here," Devlin answered, indicating the school bag on his shoulder.

George's stern expression didn't betray the surprise he felt at how little the boy had. "Okay. Well, I'll show you your room." He glanced at Aroha.

Aroha nodded and followed them both as George led the way inside.

Devlin looked around at the uncluttered interior of the spacious home. The white walls here and there displayed photos of racehorses pulling small carts. Some showed a horse in the winner's circle, surrounded by delighted, smiling people.

He followed George halfway down the hall and entered the first bedroom door. The room was furnished with a single bed and one large set of drawers. On the bed a plain, sky blue duvet cover matched curtains at the windows. The white walls were completely bare and unmarked, as if no one had ever used this room before.

Still holding his bag, Devlin went to one of the windows and looked out. His room was on the north side, facing the farmyard and distant harbour. He could see several hens ranging free, pecking at the ground.

George broke the silence. "Just leave your stuff here and I'll take you and Aroha for a walk – show you around. Okay?"

Devlin nodded. George sounded more as though he was ordering than asking. Devlin felt Aroha's description of a 'tough character' was an understatement. He felt stubbornness rising up inside him.

Carelessly he dumped his bag on the floor where he was standing and sauntered out into the hall. He ignored George's piercing, blue-eyed stare and found his way back to the lounge. He looked around at the floral lounge suite, the glass coffee table, the square bar stools at the breakfast bar and the clean kitchen. In one corner of the lounge sat a small, old-fashioned television set. Devlin looked at it in dismay. He turned to George. "Do you have PlayStation?" he asked.

George looked uncertain and glanced at Aroha for help. Aroha laughed, "It's a game. You know, like a computer game, but they can play it through the TV."

"Oh." George shook his head. "I don't have a computer, either," he told Devlin.

Devlin couldn't help looking horrified. *How backward is this man?* he wondered.

George gave his first attempt at a smile. "I'm sure you'll find you're too busy for that stuff anyway, living here." He intended it to reassure Devlin, and was surprised by the shocked look on the boy's face.

"Okay ..." Aroha cleared her throat, sensing tension rising in the room. "We'll go for that walk now, shall we? I'm looking forward to seeing the farm. Oh, George," she added, remembering, "Devlin was wondering if he could go to the hot pools sometime. I thought you might like to make it part of his schooling – part of the PE component."

George nodded, "Maybe later. He's got other stuff to learn first." He led the way out of the house. Aroha followed and Devlin came last, head down and sulking. His heart had sunk at the idea of no electronic games. *None at all?* he wondered incredulously. *What does he expect me to do all day?* Seeing days and days of boredom ahead, he only half listened as George talked, showing them the tractor shed, the gear shed where he kept all his horse stuff, the feed shed, hay barn, tying-up area for the horses, the hose-down area and so on.

Devlin eyed another large barn-type building. "What's in there?" he asked curiously.

"Two indoor training arenas," said George. "A fully enclosed round one and a full-sized rectangular one."

As they walked around a large hen house, a sandy road came into view. It curved around an oval-shaped fenced paddock where a mare and foal grazed. George explained it was the training track where he worked his racehorses.

"Will I be doing anything with the horses?" Devlin interrupted.

George nodded. "Yep. Aroha's told me you haven't had any experience, but you'll learn."

Devlin felt a bit dubious at this idea, but pretended to be cool with it.

As the three strolled back to the farm house, Aroha asked, "You okay, Devlin? Think you're going to be all right?"

Devlin shrugged.

Aroha glanced at George, "Think I might stay for a coffee, if that's okay, George?"

"Of course," George replied gruffly. "What would you like to drink, Devlin?"

Devlin shrugged again, and mumbled, "I dunno."

Aroha and Devlin sat down, Devlin with his legs straight out in front of him, slouching in the soft chair. Of all the houses he had lived in, he felt most out of place here. It was strange not to have a lady around, fussing over him. He wondered what had happened to George's wife and kid. Although George lived on his own, he appeared to keep the house clean and tidy. Devlin worried about how many chores he might be expected to do, with no one here but the two of them.

He glanced at Aroha and caught her watching him. He guessed she was afraid he would run again.

His tummy gave a loud growl. George's dog, which had plonked himself down in the open doorway, cocked his head and stared at him.

Aroha laughed. "It's been a while since you ate, eh Devlin?" To George she said, "He had a late breakfast and missed lunch. What's the dog's name?"

"That's Buster." George carried a tray towards them and placed it on the coffee table. "Help yourselves to the biscuits." He took his own mug of steaming black tea and a biscuit and sat.

Aroha took her drink and Devlin leaned forward to see what was in the third mug left on the tray. It looked like hot chocolate. Devlin decided to ignore it. He grabbed three biscuits and leaned back in his chair to eat them. Out of the corner of his eye he could see George giving him a hard stare. He didn't like the way the man seemed to be looking right into him, seeing more than he wanted him to.

Devlin stared at the carpet, flecked with white, pink

and rose. It matched the bright curtains – pastel and hot pink roses on a white background. The lounge suite was covered in the same material. Devlin thought it a bit odd – too girly. A woman must have chosen the decor. He wondered whether George had a girlfriend.

Far too soon for Devlin, Aroha finished her drink and rose from the couch. She took her keys from her pocket and smiled at him. "Well, Devlin, it's time for me to go now. George has my number if either of you need to speak to me. Just give yourselves a while to get used to things, it doesn't happen overnight. Okay?" She glanced at each of them.

George nodded and stood to follow her out the door.

Devlin frowned and stared down at the carpet. For a minute he just sat there, thinking he would not say goodbye, not bother to see her to the car. But once she had disappeared out the door, panic and fear gripped him and he leaped up and followed her. He stood a few metres from her and George as they bid each other goodbye.

Aroha turned to him and gave him a reassuring smile, waving her hand. "See you later. I'll come back and visit next week, okay?"

He watched silently as Aroha got in her car. He wanted to run and jump in beside her and beg her to take him back to Aunty Rose – anywhere but here. He remembered doing this before, begging to be taken home to his mum. He had learned it never did any good. His eyes screamed the silent plea, but pride kept him acting cool and uncaring. He shoved his hands in his pockets, refusing to wave, looking down at the dust at his feet.

The car drove away and then there was silence. Buster came and sat in front of him, looking up at him out of dark, chocolate brown eyes, asking for a pat.

Devlin ignored the dog and strode across the driveway towards the fence. As he raised his arms to lean on the top wire he heard George behind him speak a sharp warning, "Don't touch that!" Devlin pretended not to notice and brought his upper arms down on it anyway.

He gave a yell as a sharp electric jolt shot through him. He threw himself backwards, landing on his backside on the gravel.

George came and stood beside him. "That's an electric fence," he explained. He pointed out the plastic insulators on the fence posts. "The wires that go through those things are electric."

Devlin glared at him angrily and George smiled, his eyes twinkling. "That's farm lesson number one. Number two is, it pays to listen to me." He walked back to the house and added over his shoulder, "I'll go and put dinner on early, and after we've eaten we'll do the evening chores." He went into the house.

Devlin sat there feeling abandoned, empty and alone. For the first time in ages he felt tears pricking at his eyes. He began to plan his escape.

Dinner was steak, chips, eggs and spaghetti. Devlin sat at the breakfast bar and ate in silence. He enjoyed the meal but wasn't going to say so.

He followed George and put his empty plate on the kitchen bench. "You know how to load the dishwasher?" George asked him.

Devlin shook his head.

"I'll show you." George opened the dishwasher door.

Devlin made to saunter out of the kitchen.

"It's either that or you can wash them all by hand. Your choice." George fixed him with his stern, no-nonsense gaze.

Devlin reluctantly turned back to look at the open dishwasher. Together they filled it with all the dirty dishes and George pointed out where he should put the powder. Then, under instruction, Devlin set it to wash.

"That's going to be one of your regular jobs. You can load it and set it going in the evening, I'll empty it in the morning."

Devlin didn't answer. He was determined he wouldn't be staying here long enough to reload that dishwasher.

"Come on, time to go outside."

The western sky over the ocean was lit up in brilliant gold and reds by the sinking sun. George noticed him staring, "Looks good, eh?"

Devlin followed George around. He showed him how to shut the chooks up safely for the night in their hen house. They carried buckets of horse feed to the different paddocks, and filled the feed bins. They checked all the horses had water and were secure for the night. Most wore covers.

They separated a cow from her calf and made sure both were comfortable. The calf went into a sweet-smelling, bedded-down stall in the barn, where it had fresh water and would be warm. George explained the cow would give them fresh milk in the morning, before being reunited with her calf.

"That'll be tomorrow's first lesson; hand milking our house cow."

Devlin wrinkled his nose. *Gross! He wants me to milk a cow!* He said nothing, knowing he would be out that bedroom window as soon as George was asleep.

After all the evening jobs were complete, they went back inside for the night. George handed Devlin a clean bath towel. "Run yourself a good deep bath, Devlin," he ordered. "You need to soak those bruises and shampoo your hair. It looks like you've got a spot of dried blood or something in it. Let's have a look in your bag – you got clean pyjamas?"

He followed Devlin into the bedroom and watched him unzip the schoolbag. The reek of damp clothing met their nostrils. Devlin realised the wet T-shirt he had rescued from the river that morning had made everything damp.

"Pull them all out," said George.

Devlin obeyed, dumping them on the floor. Devlin's one pair of pyjamas were damp and smelly like everything else.

"You go run that bath. I'll find you a clean shirt to wear. You can pass the clothes you've got on now out the door and I'll chuck them all in the wash."

Devlin went to the bathroom. Everything in it was white and sparkling clean. He stripped, opened the door a crack and threw his clothes out into a heap on the floor. He shut the door again quickly. Looking in the large bathroom mirror he examined his bruises. There wasn't one part of his body that didn't have a blackish blue patch. No wonder he had felt sore and tender all day.

The bath felt luxurious. He stayed in it until the water had gone too cold to be comfortable.

"You shrivelled up in there yet?" George was outside the bathroom door. "Can I pass you this shirt through the door?" he asked.

Devlin got out and wrapped a large, soft towel around his waist. Then he opened the door, forgetting that George would see all his bruises. George gave no sign he had noticed, as he handed Devlin a flannel bush-shirt, saying, "There's a new toothbrush in the bathroom cupboard. Toothpaste is in there too." He closed the door again.

When Devlin returned to his room wearing nothing but the shirt that reached down to his knees, he found all his clothes had been removed from the room.

George appeared in the doorway. "I've put your clothes in the washing machine. When they've finished I'll hang them on the clothes horse in the laundry room. You can collect them tomorrow once they're dry."

Devlin stared at him in dismay. His escape plan had been ruined. He couldn't run away wearing nothing but a shirt, without any underwear.

"You may as well get off to bed, you look like you need a good night's sleep," George told him. Turning to leave he added quietly, "I don't know who gave you that beating, boy, but I can tell you there'll be none of that here. Goodnight."

He walked away.

Devlin shut the door and surrendered by crawling into bed. It felt good to be clean and lying between fresh sheets. The bed and pillow were soft and warm. He didn't hear the door open and close quietly an hour or so later when George checked on him. Devlin didn't stir all night.

CHAPTER FOUR

Devlin woke to the sound of a flushing toilet and saw that the grey light filtering between the curtains was dawn. He turned over, thinking he would go back to sleep, but instead his bedroom door was flung open.

"Time to get up!" George barked. "Morning chores first, then breakfast." He chucked a pair of men's trousers on the bed and some socks and underwear. "You'll have to make do with these today until yours are properly dry. Two minutes – I expect to see you outside. Can you hear the animals waiting?" He shut the door.

Devlin listened. Sure enough he could hear the soft lowing of the cow, keen to be milked and reunited with her baby. A rooster crowed and hens cackled. Somewhere in a distant paddock a horse neighed. He wondered what George would do if he didn't get up. He thought about that glare and decided he didn't want to find out.

Rolling out of the bed and landing on his feet, he groaned. His body felt more stiff and sore than it had yesterday. Slowly, everything aching, he dressed and stumbled out onto the front doorstep.

Buster greeted him, tail wagging furiously, the previous day's neglect forgiven. Devlin reached out his hand and touched the soft black-and-white head, giving it a gentle rub. The dog went wild with delight, bouncing around on his hind legs and chasing his tail, barking excitedly.

"Buster!" George spoke sharply, as he appeared out of the gear shed. "Settle down!" He chucked a pair of gumboots at Devlin. They landed at the bottom of the steps. "Wear those."

Devlin put them on and followed George over to the shed. George carried a clean plastic bowl. "This is for the eggs," he explained.

Together they let the chickens out of the hen house and George showed Devlin how to collect the fresh eggs. Devlin carried the fragile cargo to the house and left the bowl on the kitchen bench. Then he returned to George outside and watched him halter the waiting cow. George clipped a lead rope onto the halter and held it out for Devlin to lead her.

Hesitantly Devlin took the rope. The cow seemed to know the routine and walked willingly beside them to the tie-up area. Devlin had a feeling she didn't need the halter and lead rope at all.

George showed him how to tie the lead to a loop of baling twine using a quick release knot. "You'll get to know this real well," he told Devlin. "This is important for the horses in case they panic and pull back. You can get them untied quickly before they break their halter and, if you don't, hopefully the baling twine will break first, saving gear and horse from injury."

Next George showed him where to find the bucket for catching the milk and the stool for sitting on. They both washed their hands and the bucket and the cow's udder thoroughly. Then George demonstrated how to milk the teats. The warm milk squirted into the bucket.

Devlin had a turn and found it was harder than it looked. After a few goes he managed to get a tiny spurt of milk into the bucket. His hands ached. He listened more respectfully as George explained the technique to him again. This time he milked the cow effectively, succeeding in getting a decent amount of milk to squirt into the bucket.

George hummed gently to the cow and, after a few minutes, the milk came out more easily in big squirts. "Her milk's let down," George explained. "You're doing extremely well for a first timer." He smiled one of his rare, fleeting smiles, no teeth showing, just the corners of his mouth turning up.

Devlin felt himself responding to the praise, despite his desire not to like this man or the farm. The physical act of milking the cow gave him a strange, satisfying feeling that he hadn't felt before.

George squatted down on the other side of the cow and milked her other two teats. Together they filled the small bucket to about two-thirds full. "That's enough for us," George told him, "the calf can have her now."

He stood and picked up the bucket of milk. "I'll take this inside, you put the stool away."

Just then, the cow, impatient with the slow milking, flicked her tail. It caught Devlin a stinging whip across his cheek and eye. "Argh!" He lifted his hand to his face and stood quickly to get away in case the tail should whip again, and fell backwards over the stool.

"Oops," George looked apologetic. "We should have tied her tail. She sometimes does that, her way of saying 'get on with it'." He set off towards the house.

Devlin picked himself up and put the stool back in the shed. He listened to the sounds of the calf bleating in the stall, longing to be back with its mum. Suddenly he felt ridiculously envious. *What are you crying about?* he spoke to the calf in his mind. *You've only been separated for a night. I haven't stayed with my mum for three months!*

The peace from the early morning hand milking left him and he stood back sulkily, only half watching as George released the calf, who came bounding out of the stall. It followed its mother back to the paddock, bunting her legs and udder all the way, trying to latch on for a feed.

The next chore was feeding the horses. By the time they were finished, Devlin was well and truly ready for breakfast.

George made porridge and toast. Devlin checked out the pantry for cereals. He found only Weet-Bix. "Haven't you got any other cereal?" he grumbled rudely.

George ignored him, intent on eating marmalade toast and reading the paper.

Devlin decided to go with the porridge, which he sprinkled with brown sugar and milk. It tasted nicer than he expected. His full tummy made him feel sleepy and he yawned loudly, showing all his teeth.

"Cover your mouth when you yawn," George muttered

into the newspaper. Buster had brought the paper up from the mailbox. The box couldn't be seen from the house, so Devlin wasn't sure just how long the driveway was. He had been asleep yesterday when Aroha turned into it.

It seemed a lifetime ago. Yesterday was Monday, when he was supposed to go to school. Today was Tuesday and here he was, a long way from the city and living on a farm. He smiled at the thought of no school.

"Ready for school?" George's gruff question broke in.

"Huh?"

George stood. "I've set you up in the office. You can do your lessons and I'll do my paperwork. That way I'll be on hand if you need some help. It'll be good for me too. I'm not too disciplined at keeping up with the paperwork."

Devlin scowled, "What if I don't want to do school?" he challenged. He was afraid to look at the lessons. He had struggled so much with schoolwork. He didn't want George to see how dumb he was.

George's eyes seemed to burn brighter and sharper as he stared at Devlin. Devlin squirmed uncomfortably in his seat and looked stubbornly at the floor.

"What if I don't want to do my paperwork?" George countered the question. "It's not my favourite thing, but it feels good once it's finished. It needs to be done."

Devlin gave a rude snort.

"Schoolwork and paperwork are a necessary part of life," George said sternly. Then his voice softened. "Come on, Devlin, I've had a glance over your lessons – they don't look too bad."

"No."

There, Devlin had said it. He had defied this man. He tensed inside, wondering what would come next.

George stiffened. "Very well then, I've got an easy job for you to do instead. It doesn't require any reading or writing or maths. It's your choice."

Devlin stared at him, wondering if he was for real. He decided he must be bluffing. He stood and raised his eyebrows questioningly.

George led him outside and handed him a heavy shovel and some white sacks. "You can fill these with horse manure from the paddocks. Just be sure to keep out of the way of the horses."

Devlin's heart sank, but pride kept him from showing it. He took the shovel and sacks from George's hand and sauntered off. He smiled to show he felt he had won on the schoolwork battle front.

"Just one more thing, Devlin," George called after him, "something you might like to think about while you're shovelling. I sell those sacks for two dollars each. You can have half of that. If you want to spend the rest of your life shovelling horse manure you might just earn enough for some pocket money. But if you want to make something of your life, you can come back inside any time you like and learn something towards a career of your choice. Just remember, it's your choice." George watched Devlin walk away then went back inside.

Devlin snorted. *If he thinks I'm going to choose to go back inside, he's dumber than I thought.* He entered the nearest paddock, which enclosed a large black horse. Spying the nearest manure pat he set to work. He kept one eye on the horse, which had begun to walk closer, head half lowered to the ground. He wondered what the horse was thinking then realised it was eyeing the open gate. He hadn't bothered to latch it closed.

The horse broke into a fast trot, passing him and making for freedom. Devlin dropped sack and shovel and ran up behind the horse, intending to push the gate closed. The horse let fly with both back hooves and they landed with a smack on his chest.

Devlin fell backwards and lay there, winded. He was dimly aware of the sound of hooves clattering away up the drive and George shouting.

"Devlin! Devlin! Are you all right? Say something, for crying out loud!"

Devlin's breathing slowly returned to normal. He gasped, "Trying to get my breath."

George's face loomed over him, seeming to be turning shades of red and purple. He had looked relieved for a moment that Devlin was all right; now he seemed to be about to explode.

"Why didn't you shut the darn gate? Now my best mare has taken off up the driveway! For crying out loud, Devlin! *Always* shut the gates! Understand me?"

Devlin nodded, feeling guilty. He should've known not to assume the horse would stay where it was.

George hadn't finished. "And for Pete's sake, boy – never run up behind a horse like that! She didn't know what you were going to do – you frightened her! Horses can be very dangerous when they're frightened. You're lucky you didn't lose your head or all your front teeth. She could have killed you!" He hurried away, shaking his head and muttering, "For crying out loud! That's what I get for leaving you alone near a horse." He seized a halter and lead rope from the gear shed and headed off down the drive.

Devlin sat up slowly. He sniffed, wrinkled his nose and turned to look down at the grass where he landed. "Oh – yuck!" He had landed in a pile of fresh horse manure and now he could tell it was all through his hair and down his back. His chest felt sore where the hooves had slammed him. "Great," he mumbled, "more bruises."

A cheerful shout made him stand and look down the drive. Rounding the bend, coming to meet George, was a tall, silver-haired man leading the lost mare.

"Good on ya, Allan!" George greeted the man with relief.

"Esme was coming to meet the car," Allan explained. "I got out and caught her just before she made it to the road. How did she get away?"

"The boy didn't shut the gate," George answered gruffly. "Took a whack from her hooves, too, he did. Sent him flying onto his back. I saw it all from the hall window. Damn lucky he's not in hospital, or worse."

The two men brought the mare into the paddock and Allan and Devlin eyed each other. "Devlin, this is Allan, a good mate of mine," George made the introduction.

Devlin thought he sounded a lot calmer now.

Allan held out his hand. "Good to meet you."

Devlin wiped his manure-covered hand on his trousers and shook hands. Allan noted the shovel and sacks on the grass and Devlin's mucky appearance. "Looks like you got more on you than in the sack!" he chuckled.

Devlin gave a small, sheepish smile. He found himself liking this older man, with his broad face, kind, quick grin and twinkling eyes. Devlin had a sense the man was wise and knowing, and felt a sudden desire to have his approval.

"I put your clothes out in the sun," George told Devlin, "so they'll be dry now. You'd better go and have a shower."

The horse was made secure in her paddock once more, none the worse for her short-lived outing. The shovels and sacks were returned to the shed and the three traipsed inside.

Devlin lifted his shirt, showing the men the perfectly horseshoe-shaped bruises already colouring up on his chest. Allan whistled and George gravely shook his head. Devlin went off to the bathroom.

When he came outside again, feeling more like himself in his own jeans and T-shirt, the men were with a horse in the tie-up area. Devlin approached with caution. He had made up his mind he wasn't going anywhere near the rear end of a horse again.

"This is Betty," Allan greeted Devlin, nodding towards the horse he was brushing. "She's a red bay mare." He noticed Devlin hanging back. "She's quiet - you can come up to her."

Devlin eyed the mare warily. George handed him a

brush. "Always approach a horse near the shoulder, neck and head," he said. "I'll show you how to brush."

Devlin automatically followed George closer to the horse before he had time to think whether he actually *wanted* to be helping.

Betty gave a long sigh. Her head was down and her bottom lip drooped and quivered. She didn't appear concerned at Devlin standing close beside her. He listened as George went on instructing and began to brush her neck. Slowly Devlin worked his way down over her large shoulder.

Betty stamped her foot down on the concrete and caught his toe. "Ow!" Devlin exclaimed in pain and dropped the brush. "What did she do that for?"

"You need to stand beside her but keep your feet out of her way," George explained. "She didn't mean to stand on you, it was just a fly bothering her."

Devlin eyed the horse suspiciously. She stood relaxed, big brown eyes soft and innocent. He noticed an area of skin on her shoulder quiver, making a fly that had landed there go away. "Why doesn't she like the flies?" he asked.

"They bite," George answered, then added, "horses are very tactile; they have very sensitive skin."

"I'm about to gear up Betty and take her for a slow

work-out on the track," Allan explained, looking at him over the horse's back.

"What for?" Devlin asked. "I know some people like riding horses along the beach and stuff. Why would you want to take her around a track?" Devlin couldn't think of anything more boring, next to schoolwork.

"Betty's a racehorse – a pacer. She needs to be worked around the track as part of getting her ready for the races," Allan replied.

"Is she a thoroughbred?" Devlin asked.

"Thoroughbreds are trained for the gallops," Allan explained. "They carry a jockey on their back. The horses on this farm are standardbreds, which means they're bred to race as either trotters or pacers, pulling a driver in a sulky behind them."

"A sulky?" Devlin asked in puzzlement.

"There's one over there." George pointed to a light, two-wheeled cart beside the barn. Its long, straight shafts pointed up into the air. Its flat square seat had no back support.

"So, don't you ride your horses then?"

George and Allan shook their heads simultaneously.

"Speaking of the races," said Allan casually, "I'm going this Friday night." He raised his eyebrows hopefully at George. "Maybe you'd like to bring Devlin?"

"Is one of your horses going to race?" Devlin asked George, who had responded to Allan with a glare.

"Nope," George answered shortly. He began walking to the gear shed. "I don't race my horses anymore. I just breed them. Sometimes I help other people with their racehorses, but that's all. I don't go to the races." His voice faded as he disappeared through the doorway of the shed.

Allan smiled apologetically at Devlin. "One of these days he'll come. He hasn't been since he lost his wife and son. He gets annoyed at me asking him."

Devlin didn't have time to ask any more about it before George reappeared, carrying some complicated-looking horse gear.

Allan was bending down and picking mud out of Betty's hooves with a small tool. Devlin tensed as Allan picked up a hind leg. "Won't she kick you?" he asked.

"Nah, unlikely," Allan grunted, digging out dirt and small stones.

George heard the question. "See how he's standing beside her, not behind her, Devlin? That's so, if she does kick, he's not in the line of fire."

Allan added, "This mare is fairly quiet and used to being handled."

"I wouldn't run up behind her though," George

warned, "nor any horse, ever again."

Devlin nodded, he didn't need to be told. He had learned that lesson the painful way. Looking at Betty's strong hindquarters and muscular legs, he realised George wasn't joking about how lucky Devlin had been not to be more seriously hurt.

He continued to watch them as they placed the gear on the horse. Between them, the men explained the pieces of gear: the harness, which sat where a saddle would go, done up by a girth and attached to a crupper which the tail went through; the breastplate; the bridle, which had extra-long reins threaded through a ring on each side of the harness; the hopples, into which each leg had to be lifted and placed, and which hung from the harness; and then there were several different types of safety boots for each leg.

Next, Allan fetched the sulky and Devlin watched the men place the shafts in the correct place on the harness and secure it with long traces and shaft-ties. "How do you remember it all?" Devlin asked in wonder, thinking it all looked very complicated.

"Practice," said George simply.

"It's like anything, it's not so bad once you get to know it," said Allan. He put on a helmet and safety vest, then, standing on the left side of the horse, took both reins in his hand. Then he confidently and quietly unclipped the horse from the tie-up wall and connected the top of her bridle to the harness by something he called an 'overcheck'. Devlin noticed Betty's halter was still on underneath the bridle.

Betty stood quietly while Allan walked down and stood behind the sulky. He turned her away from the wall and, as she walked towards the training track, he got into the sulky. He sat on the ends of the reins and they poked out behind him, safe from getting caught in the wheels.

George and Devlin stood and watched Betty walk the first few metres along the track and then she broke into a faster gait.

"You see how both legs on the same side are moving forward together?" George pointed out. "That's pacing. The hopples help her to stay in that gait." He looked at his watch. "There's about an hour left to do that paperwork before lunch. You going back to shovelling?"

Devlin scowled. He shook his head.

"Schoolwork then?"

"Like you said, it's my choice," Devlin said rudely. "I choose not to do either."

"Scared since you got kicked?" George asked.

Devlin didn't answer. Secretly he was afraid to enter a paddock again, but he wasn't about to admit it.

"Here's another job then." George went to the shed and retrieved the shovel.

Devlin followed him around the side of the house to a corner of the yard. He spied a small vegetable garden, sheltered between the back of the shed and a high fence.

"I want to extend this patch to here," George indicated with his hand. "This garden does me okay, but now it has to feed you as well. You can dig it up and loosen the soil for me." Not waiting for a yes or no, he strode off to the front of the house.

Devlin leaned on the shovel, staring at the ground. *May as well, nothing better to do,* he thought grumpily. He began digging. The ground was hard. While he sweated and toiled, forming blisters on his soft hands, his mind was planning tonight's escape. He had all his clothes back in his bag now. Once George had gone to bed, he would quietly drop out of the window and be off.

This time I'll raid the pantry before I go, he told himself. *I'll go and visit Mum and my little bros and sisters.* Their faces filled his mind: his slim mother with her fine-boned face, hazel eyes and brown hair. Tracy, blonde, with her mum's hazel eyes, four years old, loving and bossy. Zachary, brown hair and eyes, three years old, so often withdrawn and quiet. A lump formed in Devlin's throat as he remembered the little boy clinging to his leg, saying nothing, but his eyes imploring Devlin either to not go or to take him too. Two-year-old Sammy, blond hair and brown eyes, round, chubby face.

Devlin smiled as he remembered how Zachary and Sammy idolised him. Zachary had practically toilet-trained himself, just to be like his big brother. Devlin had found all Zachary's clean nappies stuffed in the bin and there was no going back! *When's his birthday?* Devlin felt pretty certain it was in about three days' time. *Maybe I'll be his birthday surprise.*

The newest family member, Jade, was only seven weeks old when Devlin had last seen her on a day visit. That was when the photo he now had in his bag had been taken. He wondered what she looked like now.

Each child had a different father. His mum so far hadn't made good choices in men and none of the relationships had lasted long enough to draw any commitment from her boyfriends.

"Choices," he muttered, stopping and looking at his blistered hands. "I choose to leave this stinking place."

Hearing the clip-clop of hooves on concrete, Devlin saw Allan and Betty returning from the track. Seeing a good excuse to quit digging, he dropped the shovel and sauntered casually over to the tie-up area.

Allan nodded to him and gave him a warm smile as he got out of the cart. Devlin watched him walk up to the horse's head, undo the overcheck and clip her lead back on to her halter, securing her to the tie-up area. Steam rose off her hindquarters and patches of sweat lathered foamy white under her harness.

Devlin jumped as George's gruff voice came from behind. "Good work-out?"

"Excellent." Allan nodded. "Before you know it, Devlin, we'll have you doing all this."

"I don't think so," Devlin muttered.

George gave him a sharp look. Allan appeared not to have heard.

"We're about to have lunch," George told Allan. "You joining us?"

Allan shook his head. "Not today, thanks. I've got an appointment on the North Shore. Need anything? Groceries or whatever?"

"Yeah, there are a few things we need. I'll get the list." George strode back to the house.

Devlin leaned against the tie-up wall, scuffing the toe of his boot on the dusty concrete, making patterns.

"What about you, Devlin?" Allan asked. "Anything I can get you?"

"A PlayStation?" Devlin suggested with a wry smile.

Allan chuckled. "You'll have to save up for one of those."

Devlin shrugged his shoulders in a 'whatever' gesture. He trudged back to the house, wondering what was for lunch and longing for night to come.

CHAPTER FIVE

That night Devlin showered and crawled into bed, intending to get up again as soon as George was asleep. He found he had to fight to stay awake. After rising early it had been a long, physical day. The afternoon had brought more digging after he'd refused to help clean horse gear and the calf's stall. In the evening he loaded the dishwasher in silence, only because he was promising himself that this would definitely be the last time.

When all was quiet he slipped out of bed. His bag was ready and he dressed silently. The window opened without a sound. With quiet care that he felt would make Zorro proud, Devlin climbed out and dropped to the ground.

He wore nothing but socks on his feet, intending to stop and put his shoes on once he was out of hearing from the house. He walked silently down the driveway.

Buster, tied to his kennel, lifted his head but didn't make a sound. A shy ginger and white cat that George had mentioned he had, but which Devlin had not yet seen, ran silently past and hid under the shed. Esme the mare was watching him from over the fence. She blew gently through her nostrils. Devlin scowled.

The loose-metal driveway was lined with a wide grass verge on each side, bordered by electric fences. As he began to walk, he gazed up at the sky. He couldn't recall seeing such a spectacular sight.

Back in the city, with streetlights all around, he hadn't taken much notice of the stars. But now, surrounded by almost pitch-black darkness, the sky was a brilliant display of sparkling needle points. Then there were the millions behind, fading off into distant galaxies. He stared in wonder.

He didn't see the electric tape across the drive until he felt it press against his waist. He gasped loudly as he immediately received a jolt of electricity, sending him reeling backwards.

He glanced back at the house. No lights came on.

He peered at the tape in the darkness. It was a single

ribbon, stretching from the fence on one side of the driveway to the other. Devlin got down on the ground and crawled underneath it, taking care not to touch it again. *What's that for? Burglars?*

He trudged on. The driveway seemed endless. Glancing back he could no longer see the house. A more-pork cried out in a nearby tree, startling him. He stood on a sharp stone and winced. *Time for shoes.* Crouching down, he unzipped his bag; the noise sounded super-loud in the still night.

Suddenly, he held his breath. He had heard a snort and the ring of horseshoes on stones. He stood up, his own shoes in his hand. His heart began to beat faster. *What was a horse doing in the driveway?* Then he clicked. *The electric tape! It must be to keep the horse in!*

The hoofbeats quickened and he could see the massive, dark shape of a horse running towards him, straight out of the night.

Devlin panicked. He turned and ran in his socks on the hard stones back towards the house. Just before he reached the electric tape, he tripped and landed on his stomach. He rolled onto his back in time to see the horse rushing at him ... then it skidded to a stop, its great head looming over him, and let out a ringing neigh. Devlin cried out and covered his face with one arm. When he realised the horse wasn't going to trample him, he turned back onto his stomach and crawled as fast as he could beneath the tape.

A light came on at the end of the house. Devlin sprinted the last dash to his bedroom window and clambered back into the room. He dropped his things on the floor behind his bed and quickly got under the covers.

Seconds later his bedroom door opened. The hall light silhouetted George's frame in the doorway. "Thought I heard some noise. You all right, Devlin?"

"Yep," Devlin said casually.

"I'll just go and check on Drink-Bottle. He's an old gelding I use to settle young horses. He's grazing the driveway. Sounds a bit disturbed – unusual for him."

"Okay," said Devlin. *Drink-Bottle! What sort of a name is that?*

He heard the front door close then footsteps as George went outside. Devlin could hear him murmuring to Buster and the horses.

Quickly, Devlin got up, put his pyjamas back on and leapt back into bed. He lay, feeling upset and trapped. He decided to explore the farm a bit more and work out a better way to escape tomorrow night. Exhausted and unhappy, he drifted off quickly. He didn't hear George come back and return to his own bed.

The next morning, again at the crack of dawn, Devlin moaned into his pillow when he heard George bark, "Time to get up!"

He made up his mind to ignore him, and promptly went back to sleep. An unpleasant sensation on his back brought him violently out of slumber. With an angry and indignant yell he leapt up and shook the ice cube out of his T-shirt.

George was standing beside the bed glaring down at him. "One minute – or there'll be more ice and no breakfast." He left the room.

Devlin clenched his fists and grunted angrily as he got out of bed. The scowl on his face as he slammed the front door would have brought some sort of comment from any of his previous foster parents. But George just stood there with the cow's milk bucket in one hand and the shovel in the other. He held them both out to Devlin with a questioning look.

Devlin's mouth fell open as he understood his options. Without a word, and still scowling, he snatched the milk bucket out of George's hand and trudged towards the shed.

This time George remembered to secure the cow's tail so she couldn't flick anyone. After a few attempts, Devlin got the milk flowing well. Despite his bad start to the morning and the silence because he refused to talk to George, he secretly enjoyed milking the cow. And it felt good to receive George's nod of approval at the amount of milk in the bucket.

He tried not to envy the calf's happy reunion with its mother, comforting himself that it would soon be his turn. He wouldn't fail to get away tonight! He collected the eggs, deliberately taking a long time so that he wouldn't have to help George feed the horses.

Devlin ate breakfast in sulky silence, knowing he would be shovelling again instead of doing schoolwork. He looked at his palms, marked with blisters.

George noticed. "They'll toughen up."

Devlin didn't reply. The strained silence was broken by Buster barking and alerting them to Allan's car coming slowly up the driveway. Devlin watched out the window as Allan got out and unhooked the electric ribbon by a plastic handle at one end. The 'monster' horse of the night before was quietly licking the boot of his car. He didn't look half as big or as threatening now as he had, standing over Devlin in the dark.

Allan tried to shoo the horse away but Drink-Bottle ignored him until he was physically made to step backwards by Allan's hands on his chest. The horse stood and watched the car move ahead and then stepped forward to nuzzle Allan's shoulder while he hooked the ribbon back across the drive. Allan stooped to pick up something off the ground.

George went outside. "G'day, Allan. You get to your appointment okay yesterday?"

"Yep." Allan opened the boot of his car. "Got the stuff you wanted, too." He brought out a few shopping bags and handed them to George. He glanced at Devlin, who was now standing on the doorstep. "This yours, Devlin?" He held up a shoe.

Devlin stared at his shoe, lost for words. He felt a sudden heat in his face.

"Found it on the driveway, by the electric tape." Allan glanced at George and back at Devlin questioningly.

"Yeah, that's mine," Devlin admitted casually.

"How'd it get on the driveway?" George asked.

Devlin shrugged his shoulders innocently. "I dunno. I s'pose Buster was playing with it."

He took the telltale shoe from Allan, ignoring George's look. "Thanks, Allan." He took it back to his room then came back to the doorstep.

George handed him a new pair of gumboots, just his size. "Here you go – these are yours." Then he handed him a pair of leather gardening gloves. "And these'll help your hands. There's a lot of weeding to do around here."

"Weeding?" Allan questioned.

"The farm will be looking real tidy at the rate he's going," George replied.

Devlin pretended not to hear the comment.

"Speaking of gardening, I picked up some plants. Place was having a clear-out sale. Want to take a look?"

"Yep." George followed Allan to the boot of his car. "May as well get on with your schoolwork," George called over his shoulder to Devlin.

Devlin scowled sulkily and put on the gloves. He went off to find the shovel and left the men talking, looking into the boot of the car.

Devlin kept away from the horses and spent most of the day pulling out the weeds that grew around the edges of the buildings. He was relieved to see George move Drink-Bottle from the driveway and into a paddock. The land around the farm was steep and hilly with pockets of dark bush. The driveway looked to be the only sensible way back to the road.

His heart leapt. He had come close to getting away last night. Tonight there would be no mistakes. He enjoyed wearing his new gumboots and gloves and decided to take them with him. He would sneak the gloves into his bag and collect the gumboots from the steps after jumping out the window. Last night he had forgotten to raid the pantry before going to his room. Somehow he would need to sneak some food into a bag while George was feeding the horses their evening feed.

That night, Devlin once more pretended to go to bed. Adrenalin pumped through his veins. His bag now held crackers, apples and muesli bars. He knew that after a long time walking he would appreciate them as much as any bar of chocolate.

At last George had been in bed long enough to be asleep. Devlin silently got himself ready. Socks on his feet to silence his steps had worked well, so he did it again. Carefully he climbed out the bedroom window and dropped, expecting to land gently on the ground.

Instead he let out a yell of pain and scrambled to get away from the needles jabbing his feet and hands. Only then did he remember the conversation between the men about pot plants. Someone had put big pots of cacti directly under his window!

George's light came on. Devlin sat helplessly beside broken and scattered pots and cacti. When George came out the front door and turned on the outside light, Devlin was still sitting there, wincing with pain.

"What have you done to my pot plants?" George demanded, seeing the mess.

"Who put them under the window?" Devlin grimaced.

"Well, what were you doing jumping out of the window?" George asked. Then he spotted Devlin's bag. He strode over and unzipped it, grunting when he saw the food and clothes.

"Owww!" Devlin groaned as a sharp pain stabbed his foot again.

"Let's take a look," George said gruffly, crouching over Devlin's leg. He spotted a thorn that had broken off the cacti and gone through the sock into the sole of his foot. "Hold still." He carefully removed the thorn.

Devlin groaned, first with pain, then relief. Under the outside light he could see pin pricks of blood on his hands and they felt like they were on fire.

"Get inside and have a quick bath," George instructed. "I don't know if any of these plants will cause a reaction, so you better soak the spots where they got you. There's some antiseptic in the bathroom cupboard."

Devlin nodded and limped back inside. George took his bag into the kitchen and unpacked the food.

"What am I going to do with you, boy?" he muttered to himself.

Next morning, as usual, Devlin was woken at the crack of dawn. He felt angry and frustrated that he hadn't got away last night. He knew there was no way he would make it in time for his little brother's birthday now. His hands and feet were sensitive and tender, yet he limped across the yard to milk the cow. He didn't like to admit that he was almost looking forward to the milking.

The day passed in much the same way as the previous one. Allan came over and jogged Betty around the track. Devlin refused to go near any of the horses and whenever George was out of sight, he sat on the ground and did nothing.

George approached him at lunchtime. "Devlin, I was wondering if you'd like a pet?"

Devlin shook his head. His last pet had been a black cat. He had named it Allblack after the famous New Zealand rugby team. The cat had been deliberately run over by one of his mother's drunk, cruel boyfriends and Devlin had been devastated. He hadn't wanted another animal since. He stared at the ground.

"Well, if you change your mind, let me know." George headed inside. "Lunch time."

Later, George put Esme to graze in the driveway. "She needs a change of scenery," he said.

Devlin kept his expression blank but boiled inwardly. He wasn't game to go in with the mare again, which meant the only way to leave that night would be through bush and forest. He saw George had tidied up the pot plants and left them under the window. He hadn't mentioned the running away attempt at all.

Devlin gazed about at the countryside, across to the white caps on the Tasman Sea and the other way to the soft glint of the Kaipara Harbour. He wasn't exactly sure which direction he needed to go in order to reach the main road. He decided to go towards the Tasman Sea and hope for the best. Even if it was the wrong way, once he reached the beach he knew he should be able to follow it south. He would be less likely to get caught going that way, too. He had no idea how he would find his way through the dark green forest that lay between the farm and the beach, but he was determined to try.

That night, after dinner, when George was heading out to feed the horses, Devlin said, "I'm tired. Think I'll go to bed."

George stopped and looked at him. "No jumping out that window, okay?"

"Okay."

"G'night."

Devlin nodded.

As soon as George was out the door Devlin got his bag and packed it with clothing, gloves, shoes, food and cans of fizzy. He found a couple of blankets, rolled them up under his bedcovers to look like a sleeping body and closed the bedroom door. Then he quietly got his gumboots from the front door step and carried everything through to the back door. Silently he went out on the ocean side of the house. He knew George would be a while yet, getting the horse feed from the shed and feeding the horses on the harbour side.

As quickly as he could, he escaped through the nearest paddock, disappearing down the hill and into the first pocket of bush. Finally! He was free!

There was still enough twilight left for him to make good going through the bush. He began to relax, thinking he had won. The bush was silent and peaceful and smelt wonderfully of earth and leaves. A pair of wood pigeons fluttered in the branches of a tree above him. He gazed up at the chubby birds and, for the first time in days, he smiled.

But as darkness engulfed the bush, he felt less sure of himself. It became pitch black and he kept tripping over tree roots. He began to wonder if he was still heading in the right direction. He stopped and listened. It sounded as though there was a roar of surf to his right.

Suddenly he heard something behind him. It was making heavy, harsh breathing noises and it scrabbled up a tree, very close. He stopped and turned, tense with fear. The next moment there came a wild, hysterical screaming and screeching from above him. He looked up, terrified, and began to run backwards. Silhouetted against the night sky were two animals in full battle. They looked a bit like possums but he wasn't sure if possums made that kind of noise.

He knew it was foolish, but he kept running to put distance between himself and the ferocious fight. One minute he was running on solid ground and the next he stepped into thin air. Too late to save himself, he toppled down the side of an almost-vertical bank, rolling and tumbling, his face getting scratched by twigs and stones. The side of his head struck hard wood and still he tumbled. It felt as if he would keep rolling forever. The bag on his back provided some padding but sometimes the drink cans jabbed him sharply.

When at last his rolling stopped, he lay battered and bruised in a sorry heap. He could hear lapping water close by, which made him feel confused. He felt overcome by all the struggles of the last few days and fell asleep on the bed of scratchy grass and leaves where he lay.

George sat in the kitchen in the dark, staring out the window into the inky blackness. He had both outside lights on, one on each side of the house, so Devlin could see them in case he came back.

He thought about the phone call he had made to Aroha's mobile as soon as he discovered Devlin had gone.

"He may come home," she told him. "There's not much you can do right now. You won't be able to find him in the dark. You might be able to see where he's gone in the daylight tomorrow. I'll ring you in the morning to see if he's come back. Try and get some sleep."

George mulled over the last few days. Had he been too hard on the boy? Was he being insensitive to the boy's needs? What did he know about raising a teenager anyway? All he understood was horses.

Feeling sad and tired but unable to sleep, he went and sat on one of the lounge chairs. As the night ticked on, his head rolled to one side and he dozed.

CHAPTER SIX

George woke just before dawn. He stretched his stiff neck from side to side, then got up and went outside. Standing on the front porch he noticed the air was a crisp, predawn temperature. The sky was still dark but he felt the wind whispering the advent of the rising sun.

He grabbed his torch and first-aid kit, put on his jacket and boots, and began to walk in the direction he felt Devlin was most likely to have taken. The birds awoke and with their song came first light. Soon George could easily see the way Devlin had gone. "Like following an elephant," he muttered, eyeing the broken twigs and small plants the boy had trodden on.

As he continued he could see the places where Devlin's boots had scuffed the dirt, where he had probably tripped on tree roots. George began to feel uneasy. He knew what was ahead. He hadn't been to this spot for a long time. It hurt too much to come.

Eventually, he reached the edge of the ravine. He got on his knees and inched forward to peer over and look down the steep slope. He stared in silence and remembered his recent dream. Tears pricked his eyes.

The long, steep side of the ravine had blossomed with blue convolvulus flowers. It was a rich mass of colour, and early morning bumblebees hovered happily as if they were in bee heaven. Here and there a small shrub was thriving, taking root on the side of the slope.

At the bottom of the ravine the slope levelled off. Flowers and lush grass met the edge of the small lake, which shimmered as dawn's light danced in the ripples. Ducks quacked and paddled contentedly, sometimes dipping their heads and necks underwater for food. A black swan glided by.

Several metres from the water's edge, Devlin sat with his back to George in front of two large gravestones. The blue convolvulus had surrounded the graves in a natural carpet. Devlin was reading the inscriptions.

George slipped back and found the steep, narrow

path that wound its way down the slope. Devlin glanced up and saw him approaching, then looked back at the gravestones.

George walked up and stood beside him. He read the familiar stones in sad silence.

HERE LIES HELEN SELLECK,
LOVING WIFE OF GEORGE AND MOTHER OF GRAHAM.
GONE TO BE WITH HER LORD JESUS.
HERE LIES GRAHAM SELLECK,
SON OF GEORGE AND HELEN.
UNITED WITH HIS MOTHER IN BIRTH AND IN DEATH.
GOD BLESS THEM.

Devlin broke the stillness. "What happened?"

George swallowed the hard lump that had been forming in his throat. "The ravine," he said hoarsely. "It came down in a massive landslide. A heavy tree trunk landed on them." He nodded back towards the flowery slope. "It never used to look like that."

Devlin listened.

"The doctor said they died instantly. This was one of their favourite places on the farm. I thought they'd like to be buried here." George's eyes brimmed with tears and he blinked them away. He put his hand on Devlin's shoulder and they were both silent for a while. Then George said quietly, "I guess we have one thing in common."

Devlin raised his eyes.

"We both know what it's like to be separated from the people we love."

Devlin turned his face down to the ground and nodded. For a precious second the two felt the hint of a bond forming between them.

"Did you come down that path in the dark?"

Devlin shook his head. "Nah, I fell."

"What? You're lucky you didn't break your neck!"

Devlin nodded. He was shaken by his close call.

"Are you all right?" George asked, looking him over.

Devlin nodded again. "More bruises."

A distant mooing reached their ears as the cow expressed her feelings at being neglected.

"I want to ring Aroha," Devlin stated. "I'm not happy here. I want to go home to Mum."

George nodded. "Aroha will be ringing soon. You can talk to her then."

Without another word, they trudged back up the ravine towards the farmhouse and the upset cow.

"Yes, he's back … he wants to talk to you … hang on, I'll put him on." George handed the phone to Devlin.

"Hi, Aroha."

"Hi, Devlin, how's it going?" Aroha's voice sounded warm and kind.

"Not that great. I don't like the farm much. I hate horses. I really want to go home to Mum's."

"Do you think you've given the farm a fair trial?" Aroha asked. "I mean, it takes time to settle in to a new place."

"I hate it. I don't want to work with the horses. Why can't I go home to Mum now? Has she kicked out that loser of a boyfriend yet?" Devlin was so familiar with the pattern of his mother and her short-term boyfriends, he felt sure this time would be the same.

"No. They've been getting some counselling though, which is good."

"Is it gonna make him a better person? Can't I go back and live there?" Devlin doubted Greg would change, but he couldn't help clutching at straws.

"These things take time, Devlin." She paused. "Look, I tell you what, I'll see what other options there may be and I'll come and see you tomorrow. We'll talk about it then, okay?"

Devlin felt glum. "I s'pose."

"Pass me back to George and I'll arrange a time."

"Yep. See ya." He handed the phone back to George and walked away, shoulders slumped.

Devlin left George to it and, hearing Allan's car coming up the drive, went outside.

As Devlin watched Allan gear up his horse from a safe distance, George joined them, phone conversation finished.

"I might be leaving tomorrow," Devlin suddenly told Allan.

Allan looked startled, then disappointed. "How come?"

"Don't like it here. No good with horses. Not much else to do except dig weeds all day."

George grunted but said nothing.

"What makes you think you're not good with horses?" asked Allan.

"Just don't like 'em, that's all."

"Well, George," said Allan, "maybe you should bring him along to the trots tonight. He might think horses are a bit more interesting after he's seen the action of live Friday night harness-racing!"

George looked like he was about to snap a reply, then thought better of it. "All right." He turned and began to stride away, leaving Allan and Devlin gaping after him. George added over his shoulder, "I'll take that two-year-old along for the ride, might be a good experience for him. It'll help get him used to all the sights and sounds, without the pressure of running in a race."

Speechless that George had finally consented, Allan could only nod his head.

"I don't want to go see some dumb horse races!" Devlin grumped. He stormed off to find his gloves and boots. "Just one more night here, then I'll make Aroha take me home," he promised himself.

CHAPTER SEVEN

That evening the small horse truck rattled as George drove it carefully down the bumpy drive, mindful of his four-legged cargo. The horse gave an uncertain neigh and stamped his hooves, trying to find a comfortable way to stand.

Sitting between Allan and George in the front of the truck, Devlin kept a sulky scowl on his face. He was making it clear he did not want to be there. All three of them had showered and dressed tidily for the outing, Devlin grumbling continuously. He reminded himself that at least he would get to see the road out of this farm. That would come in handy if the worst happened and Aroha left him behind tomorrow.

As they went, he saw the way to the main road was fairly simple. Soon he began to recognise places he'd driven past with Aroha on his way to the farm. Gradually the drone of the truck motor lulled him to sleep.

When he woke, they were pulling in to the horse-truck entrance of Alexandra Park Raceway in Epsom, Auckland. George parked among the other trucks. He got out and held the door open for Devlin.

"I'm not getting out," Devlin stated stubbornly.

George paused, looking at him. "Suit yourself. Here's your ticket to get in, in case you change your mind and decide to follow." He handed Devlin a small card with a loop of string attached to it. "It's called a swinger." He showed him how to attach it to his clothing, then he fixed Devlin with a steely, warning glare. "Promise me you'll either stay here, or come and find me. No other options – understand?"

Devlin nodded. He didn't fancy another cold, uncomfortable night in the open air, anyway. He would give Aroha one more chance.

"Don't forget," Allan reminded him, "there's a good feed to be had in there. If you get hungry, come find us. I'll be looking out for you."

"And don't forget to lock the doors of the truck," George added.

The men shut the doors. Devlin heard them unload the horse from the back, then he saw them leading it through an entrance gate, following lots of other people and horses. He watched in amazement as he saw one man leading three horses all at the same time.

More trucks arrived, bringing horses, people and sulkies. Darkness swallowed the last of twilight and Devlin lay down on the truck seat, thinking he might just sleep the evening away.

He was just slipping into a gentle doze when his ears picked up some whispering. It sounded like two men were crouching down between his truck and the next, having a conversation. Devlin heard words like – "hook 'em up" and "five thousand cash" and "five in three". He wondered what it all meant. Then he heard their footsteps as they parted company.

He peeked over the top of the dash. He saw a man striding away who looked to be in his twenties, with short blond hair, wearing a white shirt and trousers. He was walking casually towards the raceway entrance. Devlin glanced in the right-hand truck mirror and caught a glimpse of a black suit as the other man went off behind the trucks.

Devlin lay back down again, but soon found that his stomach began to gnaw at him for dinner. What sort of food had he heard Allan mention to George on the way here? Roast meat, salads, hot chips and lots of desserts? Now that he thought about it, it did sound pretty tasty. Maybe it would be silly to miss out on a good feed. He didn't have to go near any horses, anyway.

With nothing but food in mind, Devlin got out of the truck. He made sure both doors were locked, before walking towards the raceway entrance. A security man glanced at his swinger and nodded, letting him pass.

Devlin followed a well-dressed lady who was leading a horse. The horse was wearing a fancy cover with the name of a race printed on the side. They entered a building which Devlin could see was lined on each side with horse stalls. People, horses and gear were everywhere. He could hear announcements coming over the loudspeakers and noticed there were television screens mounted up high inside the building, for people to watch the races.

There was no sign of Allan or George anywhere. He glanced at the horses, some tied inside the stalls, others tied outside with their hindquarters sticking out into the walkway area. He hadn't taken enough notice of George's two-year-old to be able to tell it apart from all the other horses here.

He decided to try a different tactic and cautiously approached a stall where some teenage boys were busy working. "Do you know where I can find George Selleck's horse stall?" Devlin asked a boy with a thick mop of hair.

The boys stopped, looked at each other and sniggered. The boy with the mop of hair nodded back towards a sign near the entrance with writing on it. "Can't you read?" he asked rudely. "It should be written over there."

"Nah – I can't, actually." Devlin answered in the same rude, sarcastic tone, giving the boy a glare.

He walked on and shut his ears to the quiet sniggers that followed his reply. He noticed an entrance to another section of the building, where he found yet more horse stalls. He passed someone hosing down a horse's legs and another stall where a girl was holding a horse while it peed onto the bedding straw. "Gross!" he muttered as the strong smell of urine reached his nose.

He watched someone else picking up horse poo from the concrete with a shovel and placing it in one of the specially provided bins. "Rather you than me," Devlin muttered. He turned and walked through into the second part of the building. He still couldn't see either of the men, or the horse, but finally, in a quiet corner, he noticed a small horse standing relaxed and a brown box outside its stall that looked like the one Allan had put in the truck. He was about to walk towards it when a conversation on his right caught his attention.

A small group of people were busy gearing up a tall, light-red horse with blond mane and tail. "I don't understand it," one man was complaining, "he's got the right breeding, conformation and temperament. He just doesn't run to win."

A big man in a navy suit was standing by, listening. "I know, but that's racing, ain't it?" he replied in a cold, business-like voice. "This is his last chance. I've made up my mind – if he doesn't do any good tonight you can flick him on for dog tucker. I've got other, more profitable investments to put my money into. He's cost me more than enough already."

As if he understood the man's death threat, the horse dropped his head lower and seemed to droop. Devlin noticed his eyes were soft and brown, yet they weren't bright and alert like Uncle George's horses, taking everything in. Instead, this horse's eyes seemed to be dull and introverted.

"Well, we'll soon see," the first man replied. He instructed the young girl helping him, "Get him out of the stall now, it's time to put the cart on." He looked at the big man. "Maybe you would like to go get his number for me?"

The grumpy owner went away muttering, "Useless animal," under his breath.

Devlin continued on till he reached the other end of the stable facility, where he noticed some television cameras and announcers interviewing a man. The man wore white trousers similar to the blond whisperer from the truck park.

He followed other passers-by along a path, which was separated from an arena-like area by a rail. He stopped and leaned on the rail, as others were doing, and watched a horse and driver enter the arena, fully geared up, ready to race. The driver was wearing those white pants too and Devlin realised they were part of the racing uniform. The man's jacket was a bright design of colours.

The driver began to walk the horse around the arena. Soon, other horses and their drivers followed and the arena began to fill up. Devlin recognised the 'dog tucker' horse with its distinctive height, blond mane and tail. As the horse walked past where Devlin leaned on the rail, he studied the big animal's eyes again. This time, for a long moment, the horse seemed to focus on *him*. Devlin felt as though he had read a message there but he didn't understand what it was. Suddenly he felt as if he and this horse had a connection, a sharing of circumstances that no one else could understand.

"Homeless and unwanted," Devlin whispered quietly as he watched the horse walk around the arena. "And right where you don't want to be." He noticed the number seven on the horse's side. His blond driver looked like the man he had heard whispering near the truck.

"Devlin! There you are!" He was startled and pleased to hear Allan's voice behind him. "I went back to the truck and you'd gone. Decided to join us for dinner after all?"

Devlin turned and saw Allan holding two steaming cups. He gave a small grin in reply and nodded. "Getting pretty hungry, actually," he said.

"Okay, well let's find George first. He's up the stairs here, in the stand, waiting for his coffee. We can watch this race with him then go on and have some dinner."

Devlin followed Allan up a staircase into a seating area, which was fast filling up with spectators. From up here he had a good view of the white racetrack, lit up under big floodlights. George was sitting in a row of seats, studying the race programme. He looked up as they approached and gave Devlin a curt nod and took his coffee from Allan with a gruff "Thanks."

A bugle sounded. "That means they're leaving the birdcage arena and going out onto the track," Allan explained.

Devlin sat down and watched with interest as the horses went past, pulling their sulkies and brightly clad drivers. He saw number seven getting hustled along by his driver. He noticed a lot of spectators were up at the counters, placing bets for the race. "Are you going to bet on anything?" he asked Allan and George.

Allan shook his head and George said, "No, Devlin. Money can slip through your fingers as easily as rain, if you're not careful with it. I used to place the odd bet on my own horses, when I was racing them. Not interested in getting a gambling habit though."

Allan explained, "Some people can make the odd bet, win or lose and go home happy. To them it's just a bit of fun. But sadly there are others who want to get rich quick and can fall into a nasty trap. Some people get so addicted they begin telling lies, borrowing and even stealing money just so they can gamble it. Their priorities get way out of order, and before they know it the habit is controlling them instead of the other way around."

Devlin nodded thoughtfully, absorbing all of this and everything around him. He wondered how many of the people he saw placing bets were in that predicament.

By now the horses and drivers had gathered on the far side of the track. They were walking in a circle at the starting area. In front of them on the track was a small, white truck with big gates sticking out each side, spreading across the track.

"What's that?" Devlin asked.

"That's the mobile starter gate," Allan explained. "It drives along in front of the horses, taking them around to the official start marker for the race, then it will pull away from them and they'll be racing."

Devlin watched the drivers walk their horses up behind the gate, which had begun to move slowly. As the horses locked into their positions, the starter gate picked up speed. Suddenly the race commentator announced "Racing!" and began his commentary as the mobile starter pulled away, leaving the horses and drivers battling to get themselves to the front or close to the rail.

Devlin leaned forward in his seat, looking hard for number seven and trying to listen to the race commentary at the same time. Suddenly he forgot all about Uncle George and Allan beside him and his heart was with the horse, willing it to run and try, for the sake of its life.

After the second circuit around the track a bell rang. "What's that mean?" Devlin demanded.

"Last lap," George muttered, his sharp blue eyes on the horses and drivers.

People all around Devlin began to call out to different horses they wanted to win. Some stood. One plump lady, wearing a dressy suit, bellowed, "Number four! Number four! Come on, you beauty!"

Devlin clenched his fists and held his breath as he

watched the mad sprint over the last four hundred metres. The horses spread out, trying to break through gaps to run down the leader, number four.

Number seven made its move too late and finished about sixth or seventh, Devlin couldn't quite tell.

He felt sick. *Are they really going to kill it?* he wondered. He remembered the coldness of the big man and deep down he knew it was true.

"Uncle George," Devlin began, "you remember how you asked me if I wanted a pet?"

George nodded, sipping his coffee and studying the race programme again.

"I want you to buy me that horse - number seven." He pointed at the animal, now coming off the track back towards the stable area.

Allan and George choked on their coffee. "What?" George croaked.

Allan laughed in disbelief. "What do you mean?"

"I heard a man say it was going to become dog tucker if it didn't do any good today." Devlin looked desperately at George. "You can't let them kill it. I want to save it."

George's look of amazement changed to his usual narrow-eyed glare. "If I buy it, who's going to look after it? If it's your pet, you'll have to."

Devlin nodded. "I'll look after it."

Allan glanced at George. "Come on then – no time to muck about."

Dinner forgotten, the three headed quickly down the stairs back to the stable area. Devlin led them to the box where the number seven horse was now having the racing harness removed.

George recognised the trainer and spoke to him. "Jamish, g'day!"

"George! Well, long time no see," the trainer grinned. "What can I do for ya?"

"I'm wondering if this pacer is for sale."

Jamish looked surprised then thoughtful. "Could be, actually. But he's not much of a racehorse. Don't know what's wrong with him, just not showing any promise. Doesn't seem to have it up here," he tapped his own head.

Allan asked, "What's his temperament like?"

"Quiet as," Jamish replied. "Couldn't surpass him on manners and handling. Maybe he's too quiet."

"Might make a good learner's horse for my boy here," George nodded in Devlin's direction.

"He'd be brilliant for that," Jamish agreed, eyeing Devlin curiously. "Here comes his owner – I'll tell him you want to make an offer."

The big, coldly-spoken man that Devlin had seen

earlier approached. Jamish told him, "George here wants to take this horse for a learner, to teach his boy."

Devlin held his breath nervously as the man stared at them all with cold, green eyes. George gruffly named a figure. The man thought for a bit, then nodded. "Agreed. I don't want him, I don't care where he goes. Can you take him with you tonight?"

George nodded. "Got my truck here."

"Good. The sooner he goes, the less bills I have to pay."

The horse had been stripped of everything except halter and lead rope. He stood at the cross ties, sweat dripping off his tummy, looking like he didn't care what was going on around him.

Jamish unclipped him and led him over to Devlin. He held out the lead rope for him to take.

Secretly feeling terrified, but not wanting to lose face in front of everyone, Devlin took the offered lead rope. He stood there, eyeing the huge animal, which thankfully stood quietly. *Wow! My very own horse.*

Allan smiled and winked at Devlin as he took the lead rope out of his hands. "I'll show you where we wash down the horses," he said, and began to lead the horse away. Devlin followed gratefully, leaving George to sort out the formalities.

After they had walked the horse to cool him off, they returned to the stall where George was brushing his two-year-old. George had removed the colt's warm travel rug and now placed it on Devlin's horse. "Don't want him to catch a chill," George explained to Devlin.

"I don't even know his name," Devlin commented, looking at his horse, now in the adjacent stall, towering over the younger one.

Allan opened a racing programme. "Says here his racing name is 'Brand New Tyre'."

George snorted. "He ran like he had a *flat* tyre." He looked at Devlin. "You don't have to call him that, you know. It's just his racing name. I usually have a stable name for all my horses. You can call him what you want."

Allan whistled. "Pretty nice breeding here, George." He handed George the programme for him to see. "You might have bought another bargain."

George studied the horse's details thoughtfully, then said gruffly, "Maybe, but he's not my bargain."

"George? George! Is that you?" A woman's voice spoke from behind them. They all turned and Devlin saw a woman in her late thirties, dressed in white pants and racing colours. She held her helmet under her arm, revealing light brown, sun-streaked hair, caught up in a hairnet. Her attractive face was lit with a smile, making her hazel eyes glow warmly.

"Saraia!" George sounded pleasantly surprised.

Allan spoke. "Saraia, this is Devlin. He lives with George now." Allan turned to Devlin. "This is Saraia, she's the country's top driver at the moment."

Devlin nodded. "Hi."

She smiled back. "Hi, Devlin. I used to drive some of George's horses. He helped me when I was starting out. Are you learning too?"

Devlin started to shake his head, then remembered his horse and nodded instead. "Sort of," he mumbled.

"We've just bought this horse for Devlin to learn on," Allan explained. He glanced at Devlin, eyes twinkling, "But I don't think it's quite sunk in yet."

Saraia walked forward and stroked the horse's long nose. "Mmm, he's a nice-looking chestnut."

"Chestnut?" Devlin repeated blankly.

"That's his colour," Allan explained.

Saraia raised an eyebrow at Devlin. "You really are a learner, aren't you?" she stated. "If you bring him to the races, Devlin, I'll drive him for you."

The young, blond driver who had driven Brand New Tyre in his race was walking up behind and overheard her. "What's this? Stealing my drives, Saraia?" he asked jokingly. "I usually drive this horse."

"Sure, Gallion," she answered, "but it's up to the trainer, remember?"

"There are no plans to race this horse again," George told them. "I don't train for the races anymore. He's just for Devlin."

Gallion nodded. "Okay, not much of a racehorse anyway. I'd rather drive the winners." He began to walk off, then tossed cheekily over his shoulder, "Actually, he might suit an old lady like you, Saraia."

Ignoring him, Saraia turned back to George. "I've been thinking I'd like to come and visit you some time. I haven't been out to the farm in so long. Would that be okay?"

George nodded. "Yep. Anytime."

She smiled again. "Great. I'll catch you later! Nice to meet you, Devlin … and good luck with the horse." She walked away, nodding in greeting to other people as she went.

"Well," Allan said to Devlin and George, nodding towards the two relaxed horses, "these two fellas ought to be all right here, they seem to be happy with one another. Let's go have that dinner now, shall we?"

CHAPTER EIGHT

Next morning, Devlin woke just before dawn. He lay in the dark, thinking over everything that had happened the night before. The conversation between George and Allan on the way home, while they thought he was dozing, had stirred his curiosity.

"Notice anything tonight, George?"

"Maybe."

"What do you think?" Allan pressed.

"There's so many variables in racing. Could be just coincidence."

"It's more than that, my gut tells me," said Allan.

"How can you prove it though?"

"I'll just bide my time," Allan replied. "They'll put a foot wrong sooner or later, and I'll be ready."

George nodded. "Good meal," he added.

"Mmm ... I think the boy enjoyed it."

"Yep, three helpings of apple pie and custard."

Allan chuckled quietly.

Devlin smiled into the darkness of his room, remembering. It had been a good meal, with lots of yummy things to choose from. He hadn't eaten like that – ever – that he could recall.

Once they had arrived back at the farm and stopped the truck, George made him offload the new horse. Devlin was shown how to direct the horse's head, which controlled the direction of where the hindquarters went. The horse came off quietly and easily.

They put him in a paddock with the two-year-old, seeing as the pair had already become accustomed to one another. Devlin stood leaning on the gate, watching the tall chestnut. Under the starry night sky the horse raised his head to the breeze, taking in his new surroundings. Then, to Devlin's surprise, he returned to him at the gate, blowing gently through large nostrils onto his hair, face and shoulder.

It was a special moment. Devlin felt he meant

something to this horse. He was only barely aware that a crack had opened in the protective shell over his heart. This was *his* horse. From now on they would look after each other.

Devlin got out of bed and dressed. He was about to leave the room when the door opened and George began to bark: "Time to–"

Devlin smiled at the surprised look on the man's face. "Yep."

"Good," George said simply.

Together they went through the early morning routine. They had just finished breakfast when Aroha's car pulled up next to the house. Looking out the window, Devlin sucked in his breath with pleased surprise as a little boy scrambled out of the passenger's seat. *Zachary!*

Devlin rushed out the front door. Zachary catapulted himself into Devlin's arms, nearly knocking him off balance. "Devwin! Devwin!"

Aroha followed behind. She smiled. "It's Zachary's birthday today," she explained to George who was now standing on the door step, watching. "He asked me to bring him to see Devlin. The others wanted to come too, but I said they would have to wait a little bit longer."

Devlin looked down into Zachary's chubby face. "Happy birthday, Zachary! Four today, same age as Tracy for a little while. I'm so glad I got to see you today!"

"Me too," Zachary agreed. He clung to Devlin like he would never let go. Devlin hoisted the solid little boy up into his arms.

"I haven't got you a birthday present," Devlin told the little boy, "but I do have something I can share with you." He began to walk towards his horse's paddock.

"What is it?" asked Zachary.

Devlin reached the fence. He was pleased to see the chestnut immediately stop grazing and approach them. Devlin stroked the soft nose.

"It's my horse. I got him just last night. You can share him with me, if you like."

Zachary shot out his little hand, almost slapping the horse's face as he tried to pat it. The horse didn't flinch. "A horsey! Look at the horsey, Devwin. What's his name?"

"Zak," said Devlin impulsively. "I'll name him Zak, okay?"

"But Zak's *my* name," Zachary said, unsure.

"It's to show that you share him with me, okay?"

Zachary smiled a broad, delighted smile. "Okay, Devwin! The horse can be Zak – just like me!" Then his little face grew serious again. "Are you gonna wide him, Devwin?"

Devlin eyed the horse, considering the distance from

its back to the ground. "Maybe," he answered. "I'm gonna look after him, anyway. I have to learn all about it. Uncle George is going to teach me, and Allan will too."

"Who's Uncle George? Who's Allan?" Zachary asked, looking a little scared. "Is they mean?"

Devlin smiled reassuringly. "No, they're not mean. They've been taking care of me." He put the little boy on the ground and held his hand. "Come on … let's go back to the house and you can have a biscuit and meet Uncle George."

They found Aroha already seated on the couch, sipping hot tea. "Awoha!" Zachary said excitedly, "Devwin's got a horse and it's name's Zak, like me!"

"Really?" Aroha smiled at the enthusiastic little boy. She raised her eyebrows to Devlin, asking for an explanation.

Devlin wasn't sure what to say, so he said nothing. Instead he got his little brother a biscuit and a drink of rich, creamy milk. "I milked this from the cow early this morning," he told Zachary.

Zachary's eyes opened wide in wonder at this information. The milk was warm, still cooling after being heated on the stove. He drank it with relish and grinned an appreciative milk-moustached smile at Devlin.

George was sitting on a stool at the breakfast bar, observing them quietly. Zachary noticed him but looked too uncertain to say anything.

"Well, Devlin," Aroha began, "I've been considering your unhappiness here. It's not a good time for you to return to your mum, but Aunty Rose is keen to have you back. You'd have to face the schooling issues though."

Devlin shook his head. "No."

"You *have* to go to school, Devlin; that's the law."

"No, I mean, no, I don't want to go to Aunty Rose. I – I want to try here a bit longer."

Aroha's eyes opened wide in surprise. "But I thought – you sounded so upset on the phone yesterday ..."

Devlin nodded. "I was. But now I have a horse, all of my own. I've promised to look after him. He and I have to stay here for now."

George nodded silently, his stern expression betraying nothing of his thoughts.

Aroha looked from one to the other. "Well – that's a sudden change of heart. But I'm pleased." She took a deep breath as she adjusted herself mentally to this new turn of events. She smiled. "You'd better show me this horse, then."

Zachary leaped off the couch where he had been snuggling beside Devlin. "I'll show you, Awoha! I'll show you the horse. Me and Devwin – we're share-wing him."

Together the group walked outside. George fetched a

halter and lead-rope and caught the horse for Devlin. He led him out into the yard, closing the gate to keep Zak's two-year-old paddock mate safe within.

"Can I wide him? Pwease?" Zachary turned imploring eyes on his big brother.

Devlin looked at George.

"You lift him onto his back and hold onto him tight – don't let go," George instructed. "I'll lead you at a quiet walk. Should be all right."

Devlin did as he was told and held on firmly to Zachary's waist, while walking alongside the horse. George led them in a circle around the yard.

Zachary let out whoops of excitement and pleasure, patting the horse vigorously. Zak moved quietly, unperturbed by the excited child on his back.

After another circuit, Devlin offered to show Zachary the chickens and the cow and calf and the rest of the farm. The little boy reluctantly allowed himself to be removed from the horse's back and they watched Uncle George return him to his paddock. Then he skipped happily off, hand in hand with Devlin, chattering about everything he was hearing, seeing and experiencing.

An hour later, Aroha buckled one sad little boy into the booster seat in her car. Devlin felt wretched as he saw the tears spilling from the little boy's eyes, even though he had hugged him and promised that he could come back again very soon. As the car bumped away down the drive, Devlin had that horrible, cold, empty feeling of loss once more. Part of him was bumping away down that drive.

It was then that he made the first real decision in his life. Somehow, somewhere, he was going to provide a home for Zachary and the rest of the family. It would be *his*. Devlin's home. He would make the rules – and the first would be that none of his mother's rough boyfriends were welcome.

He would take care of Tracy, Zachary, Sammy and Jade, and his mother too if she wanted. They would live together on a farm like this one and Devlin would teach them how to get the eggs and care for the cow and …

A firm hand on his shoulder interrupted his thoughts. "He's a great little boy," George told him.

Devlin nodded. "Uncle George, I want to own a farm like this one," he said. "I want to have a place where he and the others can come and stay forever."

George squeezed his shoulder lightly. "You can, and you will," he said gruffly. "Just keep your goal in mind and go at it. But that brings me to one more problem we've got to solve."

Devlin looked at him.

"School."

Devlin looked down at the ground.

"Allan suggested something you might like to consider. It's an incentive. One full term of schoolwork in return for the cost of keeping your horse, and a PlayStation at the end of the term."

Devlin met George's eyes again, taking in his words and their meaning.

"You still have to keep up with the other jobs, and the gardening and weeding, as well as working with your horse."

Devlin felt weary at the thought of it all.

"You want to achieve your goal, don't you?" George challenged. "Believe me, doing your schooling will make it a lot easier."

"I – I can't," Devlin confessed. "I'm no good at it. I'm dumb."

"Well, I think you can let me be the judge of that," George told him. "I haven't seen anything dumb about you yet. Ignorant maybe. Not dumb. Ignorance just comes from lack of education. What colour's your horse?"

Devlin frowned, puzzled at the question. "Chestnut."

"Nothing wrong with your memory, nothing wrong with you at all," George stated. "The only thing dumb about you, is you thinking you are dumb. Start telling yourself the truth – that you are an intelligent young man with a goal to achieve."

Despite George's words Devlin felt panic tightening his stomach as he considered approaching the school desk on Monday. "What if you're wrong? And I can't learn?" he asked.

"Think about what you've already learned this past week," George ordered. "Education isn't just about what's on paper. Trust me."

Devlin tried to absorb this but couldn't squash the upset feeling in his stomach. Then he decided not to think about it again until he had to.

He enjoyed the rest of the weekend: catching Zak, tying him, cleaning his hooves and brushing him, learning the little things about this basic routine from George. The horse proved to be as quiet as his trainer had promised and Devlin's confidence in being around the animal grew stronger.

Monday came and Devlin faced the moment he dreaded. He sat down at the desk in George's office and waited, still feeling sick at the thought of failure.

George placed pen and writing paper in front of him and a piece of blank paper as well. "Write something for me about your horse," he ordered. "Then I want you to draw me a picture of him on the blank paper. Don't worry about mistakes, just do your best."

Devlin decided that didn't sound too hard, so he wrote down the things he had learned about caring for his horse. He knew his words were messy and spelt wrong. Then he drew a picture, but it looked more like a blobby donkey than his horse.

The sickness in his stomach began to ease when George praised him for a great effort. Then he was given an easy book to read, right back at beginner's level. Then there were some basic adding and subtraction problems to do.

"Right. That's it for today." George gave a small, satisfied smile. "Well done."

Devlin felt surprised at how the time had passed so quickly.

"We're just starting off slow and easy," George explained. "When you're ready, it will become a little more challenging, but I'll do my best to make it fun. You okay with that?"

Devlin nodded. He felt as if a huge burden was lifting off his shoulders.

"Time for lunch, then another lesson with your horse," George stated.

Devlin was surprised to find himself really looking

forward to catching Zak again and spending some more time with him. Maybe he would become a real horsey-person after all!

"Today you can learn about putting on the harness, the different parts and what they're for," George was saying, standing beside Devlin and Zak at the tie-up area. "I'll show you how each piece goes on, then I'll take it off and you can have a go."

Devlin listened and watched carefully. He was impressed with Zak's patience as he clumsily tried to place the pieces of harness in their correct positions. Zak received bit and bridle with no fuss. He and George went over the process again and again until Devlin was doing it competently, in the correct order.

Allan arrived and watched a demonstration by Devlin of what he had learned.

"Excellent. You can gear up Betty for me now."

Devlin did what was requested, managing once more to achieve the task competently. Then he stood back and watched Allan and George put the cart on, ready for Allan to jog her round the track.

"Wouldn't hurt for you to give Devlin's horse some exercise," George told Allan. "Just take him with you on the lead."

Devlin watched Allan walk Betty onto the track, managing the reins and Zak's lead rope at the same time. Zak eagerly broke into a trot as soon as Allan clicked at Betty to move faster.

"That's good, he's not pulling back at all," George commented, standing beside Devlin and watching Zak co-operate with Allan.

Devlin nodded.

"Tomorrow we may as well put a cart on him and see what he's like to handle on the jogging track. After that, it'll be your turn to learn to drive him."

Devlin nodded again, feeling a mixture of nerves and excitement. He was really going to get to drive his own horse!

That night he went to bed worn out from the busy day but feeling more content than ever. He drifted off to sleep, imagining what it might feel like to be in control of Zak on the jogging track. He decided to ask George if he could learn to ride on the horse's back as well.

CHAPTER NINE

The next day Devlin had another positive school session. George was being true to his word and taking Devlin slowly, finding out what level he was at in each subject. Devlin began to relax. He found it was a relief not to have any other students to distract him or make him feel dumb. It was great having Uncle George's undivided attention every time he needed him for something.

"Ya know something?" Devlin said at the end of lesson time.

George raised his eyebrows. "What?"

"This isn't so bad, after all."

George nodded and gave one of his fleeting smiles. "And it's only going to get better," he replied. "Hungry?"

After lunch, Devlin caught Zak and gave him a vigorous grooming. He cleaned out his feet, remembering in which direction to use the hoof pick, and how to stand safely while doing it. Then he geared him up with bridle and pacing harness, feeling chuffed that he still remembered how to do it correctly.

George had been observing it all quietly. "Excellent," he said simply. "Now for the leg protection." He pulled some things that resembled skateboarder's kneepads out of a box. By the time they had finished putting kneeboots, shinboots and bellboots on Zak, he looked like he was wearing enough armour to go into battle.

George led Devlin over to where the carts were stored and Devlin brought one back to his horse.

"Make sure you line it up properly first before you bring it forward," George instructed. "You don't want to poke the horse with one of the shafts. Bring it up behind him straight. That's it – now hold one shaft and put it through the carrier loop here. There, that's it. Now we do this ..." George wound the traces – long strips of leather from the breastplate of the harness – around the shaft a few times, until he had nearly reached the driver's seat. Then he hooked it over a specially made piece of metal on the shaft. "Now the other side."

Devlin copied George, winding the leather trace down

the other shaft and hooking it securely. Next, George showed him how to put the cups on – moulded plastic pieces, covering the pointed ends of the shafts. The cups were connected to the harness by short leather straps. "That's to help stop the shafts from going too far forward, and to protect the horse from getting poked," George explained. Then he showed Devlin the tie-downs, which secured the shafts in place.

"Where are the reins?" Devlin asked, suddenly realising there were none attached to the bridle.

"They're kept separately," said George. He got them out of the harness storage container and handed one to Devlin.

Devlin held the long piece of leather in his hands. George demonstrated with the rein he held, attaching it to the bit ring and threading it back through a metal ring on the harness then resting the end of the long strap on the driver's seat. Then Devlin did the same with the rein he had on the other side of the horse.

Devlin stood back to observe the harnessed horse. "Where's Zak gone?" he joked. "He's so covered up, I can hardly see him."

"I'll check the boots for scuff marks after I've jogged him," George explained. "I'll be able to see if he's hitting himself anywhere. He may not need to wear them for jogging. We'll see. I may decide to alter his shoeing."

"Do you use a blacksmith?" Devlin asked.

"Usually called a farrier these days. Nope – I do it myself," George answered. "Had plenty of experience. My father did it for a living, and I learned it from him."

George put on a safety vest and helmet and instructed Devlin to stand back a little. Devlin watched as George held both reins and at the same time unclipped the horse's head. Zak moved his head, looking expectantly at George, but stood patiently as his overcheck was done up. George walked quietly back and stood behind the cart. He let the horse stand for a moment before gently pulling on the rein to turn him to the right. Zak responded and went where George directed, walking towards the track.

After a few paces, George nimbly hopped into the cart, taking care to sit on the ends of the reins so that they didn't get caught in the wheels or drag on the ground. They walked a few metres onto the track then, on command, Zak broke into a relaxed jog. Devlin watched as they got further and further away. Zak didn't seem to be giving George any trouble.

Twenty minutes later, George and horse returned to the tie-up area. "Good as gold," said George. "Shouldn't give you any problems. Tomorrow we'll gear up the two-year-old as well, and I'll jog along beside you. Now let's get everything off him."

That afternoon a phone call from Aroha surprised Devlin. "I've arranged to bring your mum and the kids out for a visit on Saturday. Think that'll be okay with you and George?"

Devlin checked with George, then replied, "Sure, that's okay. What time?"

"About ten-thirty Saturday morning? Great! We'll see you then! Oh – how's the horse going?"

"Good."

"And the schoolwork?"

"Okay."

"I'm very pleased to hear that, Devlin. All right, we'll see you on Saturday."

"Thanks, bye."

"I'll be able to show Mum my horse," Devlin told George with excitement, "and you'll meet Tracy and Sammy and Jade – she's just a baby. Zachary will be happy to come back too."

George nodded. "We might have to do some cooking on Friday then. Treat them to some farm baking."

"Can I choose what to make?" Devlin asked.

George nodded again.

"Cool."

"I'm not much of a baker," George added, "but between us I'm sure we can figure it out."

Devlin nodded, grinning. "I reckon."

The following afternoon, Devlin's nerves and excitement mounted. He was going to drive his horse today! He wondered how fast they would go. He brought Zak in to the tie-up area and went through the normal routine, grooming, cleaning and gearing up.

George caught the two-year-old and did the same thing.

"What's that one's stable name?" Devlin asked.

"I call him Rimu," George answered. "I want him to grow big and strong like the tree."

As soon as Rimu and Zak had carts on and were ready to go, George put on his helmet and safety vest, as did Devlin. Then he made sure Devlin was seated safely in the cart, instructing him on how to get in and how to hold the reins. "Don't drop them," he warned, "but if you do, don't panic – just pick them up again."

He went through the rein signals for go forward, left, right and slow down. As soon as he was satisfied Devlin had understood, he said, "Ready?"

Devlin nodded, holding the reins and sitting on the seat with his feet in the footrests of the cart.

George unclipped Zak, did up his overcheck and held the horse's head while Devlin turned him towards the track. Then George let him go and went back to Rimu.

Allan arrived in time to watch them both leaving the tie-up area.

Devlin kept Zak at a walk until George and Rimu had come alongside him on the jogging track. It felt a bit strange to sit in the sulky, with nothing behind his back for support. He let the reins go a bit slack.

"Tighten up the reins slightly," George told him. "You want to be able to feel gentle contact with the horse's mouth, or close enough that you know you can have control in an instant."

Devlin made the adjustment.

"You ready to jog now?" George asked.

Devlin nodded.

"Okay, just give a gentle tug, alternately on each rein, enough to tell the horse you want him to respond."

Both Zak and Rimu quickened and began pacing. Devlin was unprepared for the sudden surge forward and his upper body went backwards. He managed to keep hold of the reins and stopped himself falling out of the cart. Then he leaned forward slightly, feeling less precarious in his seat that way.

"Okay?" George asked.

Devlin nodded.

"We'll just jog along quietly like this for a while. Always watch ahead to see where your horse is going. Be careful not to let him run too close to me and Rimu, or he'll push us off the track. I think you'll find he's okay. He knows what he's meant to do."

George was right. Zak behaved sensibly as they jogged round and round the track alongside George and Rimu. He felt another surge of warmth towards his horse, grateful that Zak made him feel so safe. He enjoyed the slow work-out immensely, taking in everything he was learning from the horse and from George.

Finally, they slowed down to a walk, just in time to see Allan and his horse Betty walking onto the track for their work-out.

"How was it?" Allan called out to Devlin.

"Great!" Devlin nodded.

"See you soon, then." Allan clicked his tongue at Betty and she jogged away down the track.

Devlin and George returned their horses to the tie-up area. Zak stood patiently and Devlin stayed in his seat and waited while George clipped up Rimu and then Zak.

Then he set about getting the cart and everything else off his horse. Zak had got up a slight sweat, so Devlin washed him with the hose. He laughed when the horse tried to catch the hose with his teeth to get a drink.

"Here's a cover for him," George said, bringing a horse cover out of the shed. "I'll show you how to put it on and do up the clips."

Soon Devlin returned Zak to his paddock. The horse came back to him at the gate and whiskered his face. "Thanks for a good lesson, boy," Devlin whispered. "You're a good teacher. You can teach me everything you know and maybe we'll learn some new things together. Might even put the sparkle back in your eyes."

Devlin had noticed his horse's eyes still had that deep, almost withdrawn look. He wondered what was causing it and made a mental note to ask Uncle George. He went off to find his gloves to do some more weeding.

Over dinner, Devlin asked shyly, "Have you noticed Zak's eyes, Uncle George?"

"What about them?"

"They don't seem to have the same spark in them as your horses."

George thought for a moment. "Hmm ... now that you mention it, I think you're right." He gave Devlin an impressed look. "You'll make a good horseman, you know. Keep up the good work."

"But what does it mean? His eyes?"

Again George pondered the question. "It's sometimes a sign they're not a hundred percent well – or perhaps in pain. Or it can be that they just need a break."

"Would a vet be able to tell us?"

"Maybe. But Jamish, his old trainer, said he'd had him thoroughly checked out by the vet. Nothing wrong anywhere."

"What else can we do for him then?"

"Could be that with some variety in his training, and lots of love and care, he'll just perk up."

"Would he let me ride him?"

George raised his eyebrows. "You want to?"

Devlin nodded. "I thought it might be fun to explore the forest and ride on the beach," he explained.

George gave a curt nod. "Let's see this week out first, practising everything you're learning on the track. Then, next week, we'll take him to the indoor arena and have a different kind of lesson."

Devlin's heart leapt with excitement. He was going to sit astride Zak and they would both learn something new! He hoped that Zak would like it. It might even put some life back into his eyes. Variety – that was what Uncle George had said. With a pleasant jolt, Devlin realised his main life-focus had changed from caring about himself to caring about his horse. It was beginning to give him a sense of purpose. That, and his long-term goal to have a farm of his own.

Before drifting off to sleep that night, he daydreamed about Zak: riding him through the forest, galloping along the beach – maybe even winning at the races. How much money did the winning horse owner get, anyway? Could Zak help him achieve his goal of owning a farm? How old did a person have to be to own property? Mulling over these questions, Devlin drifted off into a deep sleep.

CHAPTER TEN

Friday came and Devlin's school lesson was food technology – the cooking lesson.

"I want to make a chocolate cake for the kids," Devlin told George, "and fudge for Mum. She likes fudge."

"Okay, what about some pikelets as well?"

Devlin nodded. "Have we got all the stuff we need?"

"Allan did some shopping for us yesterday," George answered. He opened a recipe book and frowned at the instructions. "Maybe I should have asked him or Jackie to do this," he muttered. He read out loud. "It says – 'cream butter and sugar'. Lucky we've got all of those. I didn't know chocolate cakes needed cream, though. Must be a way to make it rich and moist."

Devlin nodded. No one had ever taken the time to teach him to cook before.

"Here's the measuring jug." Devlin took it out of the cupboard from where he had seen it stored.

"Okay, we'll use that for the dry ingredients. It says here how much we need."

"How much cream?" Devlin asked, getting it out of the fridge.

"That's strange … doesn't say. Silly recipe," said George.

"I'll just pour in the whole bottle, then?"

"Well, try half for starters – hopefully that'll be all right," George conceded.

Devlin poured the cream into the mixing bowl. Then he added the butter and the sugar. He mixed it all as much as he could, but the butter was hard and it all ended up a bit lumpy.

Then they measured the cocoa and flour in the measuring jug and added that and the last of the other ingredients into the bowl. It became a brown, sloshy mix with yellow lumps.

"Looks a bit strange, doesn't it?" George said, peering into the bowl.

"Shall I put it in the cake tin?" Devlin asked.

"Yeah, go on. Maybe it'll look better once it's done.

While that's cooking, we'll have a go at the fudge."

Devlin placed the cake tin in the oven, then set out the next ingredients he needed for the fudge. The kitchen bench was a cluttered mess of disorganisation, with patches of spilt ingredients and dirty utensils.

A knock at the door surprised them both. "That you, Allan?" George called. "You know you don't need to knock!"

The door opened and the breeze brought in a faint scent of perfume. "It's only me!" a female voice called. "I was calling on someone with a horse in this area and thought I'd chance a visit. Okay to come in?"

"Saraia!" George exclaimed. "Of course. Come on in."

She kicked off her boots at the door and came in to the kitchen, immediately taking in the scene. "Cooking?" She had a quick glance in the oven. "What's that?"

"Chocolate cake … or it will be," said George. "We didn't know how much cream to put in, so I think it's a bit sloshy."

"Cream?" Saraia picked up the open recipe book and looked at the recipe. "Where does it say cream?"

"Right there," George pointed at the instructions.

She hooted with laughter. "Ah – looks like I got here just in time." She spied the measuring jug. "I s'pose you used this for all the dry ingredients?"

Devlin and George nodded. Her amused look increased.

"Why?" Devlin asked shyly.

"Okay. For starters – to *cream* the butter and sugar is something you *do*, not an ingredient. And you need kitchen scales to weigh the dry ingredients – this jug won't give you the right weights. Sugar weighs differently to flour – right?"

George nodded. Devlin said, "Uh-oh."

"We'll let your cake cook and see what happens. But maybe we ought to start again?"

"Yep. Sounds like a good idea to me," George agreed. "I'll just skedaddle and leave you to be cooking instructor for today."

"No way," Saraia said firmly. "It's not going to hurt for you to learn as well. You're staying put, mister."

George blinked. Devlin wanted to laugh. He hadn't seen George get bossed around by anyone before. Luckily George's manners won through and he said reluctantly, "I s'pose."

Devlin enjoyed the rest of the lesson. Saraia turned out to be a good, patient teacher. By the time the morning was over, they had one odd-looking, gooey chocolate cake, which had sunk in the middle, one perfect one, a tin of fudge and three plates stacked with pikelets.

George and Devlin had learned a lot. "Thanks, Saraia, you've been a great help," said George.

Devlin nodded his agreement.

"Like to stay for lunch?" asked George. "Creamy, sunken chocolate cake our specialty, with maybe a pikelet or two on the side?"

Saraia laughed. "Okay, I guess I won't die if I try a bit of your cake. You working any horses after lunch?"

George and Devlin nodded. "You want to jog a two-year-old for me?" George asked. "You can tell me what you think of him."

Saraia nodded. "All right."

"You'll be working alongside Devlin and his horse," said George. "Might be nice for him to have a different instructor for a change, too."

Saraia smiled at Devlin. "Sure. How's it been going, Devlin?"

Devlin nodded and answered shyly. "Great. Zak's really good to learn on."

There was a sound of someone else kicking off their boots at the door and Allan entered.

"Ah – you must have smelt our wonderful chocolate cake cooking!" George accused him.

Allan eyed the cake with the sunken middle. "I dunno about that."

"Have some lunch," George ordered, "then you can work Betty alongside Saraia and Devlin later."

"Don't mind if I do," said Allan, pulling up a chair at the breakfast bar. "At least the pikelets look edible."

Devlin grinned. "That's my plate there," he pointed at his stack of pikelets. "Tell me if I passed my cooking lesson."

"Certainly," said Allan, grabbing a knife and some butter. He turned to Saraia. "Races tonight."

She nodded. "Yep. I've got a full card tonight. Driving every race." She looked at Devlin and George. "You guys coming?"

George opened his mouth to reply then caught the hopeful look crossing Devlin's face. "Well … " he paused, "I s'pose … if Devlin really wants to, we can."

Devlin nodded. "Yeah, that'd be cool."

Allan looked smug.

"It's more learning for you, I s'pose," said George, glaring at Allan. "That's the only reason we're going."

"And the food," Devlin added. They all laughed.

Devlin and Zak moved onto the track, jogging alongside Saraia and Rimu. Allan and Betty brought up the rear. Devlin noticed Betty was following so close she had her nose right on Saraia's shoulder. Saraia didn't seem bothered in the slightest. "That's what it's like in the races," she explained to Devlin when she noticed him looking. "The horse behind often breathes down your neck. They can sound pretty loud in your ear, especially when they're running hard out. You get used to it, though."

Just for demonstration, Allan moved Betty over so that she was following behind Devlin. At first he felt tense that her nose was so close to his shoulder, but after a while, when nothing had gone wrong, he relaxed.

"Your horse is a lovely mover," Saraia observed. "Pity he doesn't race to win."

"He might, later," said Devlin. "I'm going to learn to ride him and give him some new things to think about. It might put some spark into him, don't you think?"

"It might … doesn't hurt to try, anyway. I'm just going to make this young fellow move along a bit quicker now," she told Devlin. "You keep a hold of your horse, or he might try to come with me, okay?"

Devlin nodded and tightened his fingers on the reins. He was now used to holding them the correct way and felt confident he could control his horse.

Rimu began to pick up speed. Zak's ears flicked backwards and forwards and he automatically began to pick up as well. Devlin took hold of him but was surprised to find it more difficult than he expected. He soon found his horse pulling him a lot faster than he'd jogged so far, keeping up with Rimu easily. They left Allan and Betty behind.

After a few minutes, Saraia slowed down. She laughed merrily. "Harder than you thought to hold him, eh?" she asked.

Devlin nodded.

"I must admit, I didn't expect him to be so keen, myself. You managed the pace well, Devlin. You'll have to be more firm with him next time though. You don't want him thinking he can just take off when he likes. You need to be in charge."

Devlin nodded again.

"I tell you what, let's try again. Take a firmer hold of him and really mean what you're saying, okay?" She clicked Rimu on and the little horse sped up once more.

Devlin gritted his teeth and held on to Zak more firmly. This time his horse kept pacing at the slower speed. Saraia and Rimu left them behind and presently Allan and Betty caught up to him and drew alongside.

"Well done," said Allan. "You got it the second time. You'll find going to the races tonight a bit different from last week, I think, because you've learned a lot this past week – in all sorts of ways."

Devlin looked at him questioningly.

"Last week you were an upset, grumpy young lad. This week you'll be looking at everything through the eyes of a budding horseman. It'll be different, you'll see."

That night, Devlin did see what Allan meant. He had come a long way in just one week. Walking past the horses having their gear put on or removed, he could see what was happening with a much clearer understanding.

Zak's old trainer noticed the group walking by and nodded towards them. "George. How's that horse going?"

"Good as gold. Just like you said."

Allan added, "The lad's been learning a lot with him."

The trainer looked satisfied with this reply and continued gearing up the horse he had in the crossties.

"Any chance?" Allan asked suddenly.

Without looking up, the man gave a small smile and a curt nod.

Suddenly Gallion appeared, obviously the driver once again. The three observers quietly walked on.

"Well," said Allan thoughtfully, once they were out of earshot, "I'll be interested to see how that one goes."

George simply nodded.

Allan opened the race book to the coming race and traced his finger down the list of horses, looking for the trainer's name. "Here it is – number five, Stir Fry – and Saraia's driving number seven, Smooth Buttercup." They headed up to the stand to sit and watch the race.

Saraia drove an expert race and the three observers stood and cheered as she won with Smooth Buttercup.

"Glad I'm not the one with my money on that horse tonight," George commented when number five came in second to last.

"Huh!" Allan said, frowning. "Stir Fry was meant to be a sure threat to the favourite. If anyone ignored it, picking the trifecta would have been made a little easier."

"What's a trifecta?" Devlin asked.

"You have to pick first, second *and* third," Allan answered. He returned his attention to his racebook. "D'you think that driver gave it everything?" he asked George without looking up.

"Hard to say," George grunted. "I'd sure be asking him for an explanation before I'd put him on one of mine."

"But why wouldn't he give it everything?" Devlin asked.

"That's a good question, Devlin," Allan said, "a very good question."

Devlin watched the losing horses exit as Saraia brought Smooth Buttercup into the winner's circle. The desire to drive a racehorse on this track and find out what it was like, took hold of him. *Could we bring Zak back to the races?* he wondered. *First I've got to find out what will make him really want to win.*

Devlin rushed around on Saturday morning, finishing all his chores ready for his family's visit. As the time crept nearer, he kept glancing up the drive, hoping for the sound of Aroha's car.

When she did arrive, it was behind the wheel of a multi-seater van. Devlin could see his mother sitting in the front passenger's seat, smiling and waving, as they came up to park in front of the house.

Both women were wearing dark glasses and Aroha pushed hers up onto her head as she climbed out of the vehicle. "Hi there!" she greeted Devlin, who was walking out to meet the van, and George, standing on the front steps.

"Cool van!" Devlin replied.

"Yes – my car doesn't have enough seatbelts, so I had to borrow this one for today," Aroha smiled.

Devlin opened the door for his mother and then slid open the back door.

"Hi, honey." His mum opened her arms as she climbed out, taking him into an embrace. "So this is where you're living now?"

Devlin returned the hug and gave her a strong squeeze. To his surprise she winced. He stepped back, unsure. "Are you all right?" he asked, trying to read her eyes through her dark glasses.

She managed a laugh, which sounded slightly fake to Devlin. "Yes – you must have developed some muscles since you've been here!"

"I suppose I might have – I've been working lots," Devlin replied. Then the clamouring children diverted his attention and he turned to help them out of the van.

Zachary was the first one out. Being familiar with everything from his last visit made him eager and unafraid. Devlin picked him up and swung him around. Then he turned to coax Tracy out. She was looking at him warily, as if to check it was really him. "Come on, Trace," he smiled, arms outstretched.

Suddenly convinced, she threw herself into his arms. He gave her a hug and put her down gently. She wouldn't let go of his hand.

With only one hand free, he offered it to Sammy, who was climbing out of his car seat. Sammy took it and jumped to the ground, looking at his surroundings with curiosity.

Jade had fallen asleep in her car seat. Devlin gazed down at her pale face. She had developed into more of a baby, less a newborn infant. "How old is Jade now?" he asked his mum.

"Four months. I'd like to let her sleep for a while. Enjoy the peace while I can," his mother stated with a wry smile.

Devlin looked at her. The sun brought out the cherry-red glow in her hair, and he thought how wonderful it was to see her again. *Without the boyfriend*, he added mentally. He suddenly felt shy and awkward, aware once more how much he had changed since he had come to this farm.

"Why don't you take everyone for the grand tour?" Aroha suggested. "I'll have a chat here with George and keep an eye on the baby."

"I'll show them!" said Zachary importantly. "I already know where everyfink is!" He led the way to the chicken coop, while Tracy and Sammy swung on each of Devlin's hands, skipping and hopping with excitement. Their mother walked beside them.

Zachary remembered everything well, ending the grand tour at Zak's paddock. "That's our horse," Zachary announced proudly, "the one named Zak, after me."

Tracy looked sulky for a moment. "Devlin," she said tugging on his hand, "will you name a horse after me for my birthday?"

"I can't promise it yet," Devlin replied with a small smile, "but one day I'll try, okay?" Tracy nodded, somewhat satisfied.

Zak came over to the fence, curious about the party of onlookers. He sniffed at Devlin's mum's face, bumping her sunglasses so that they went crooked on her nose. "Oh!" she cried and quickly put them straight.

Devlin's mouth went dry. "Mum," he said in a low, gentle voice, "why do you have a black eye?"

She looked upset and embarrassed at the question but laughed in reply. "Oh, you know me, clumsy as always."

Devlin thought about it. "Not really," he said, watching her expression carefully.

"Oh, don't be silly. I just banged myself on the corner of a cupboard door, that's all."

Devlin didn't believe her, but said no more while they were patting his horse.

As they turned to walk back to the farmhouse, Devlin said casually, "I had lots of bruises the first week I was here." When she didn't reply he continued. "I ran away from Aunty Rose and got beaten up by a street gang. Then, when I first came here, I got kicked by a horse – and then I fell down a bank."

"Sounds like you've really been in the wars – even more than me," she said in a light tone.

"Wouldn't you like to live on a farm like this, Mum?"

She thought about it. "Mmm ... yes, I think I would."

Devlin hesitated for a moment, then his desires rushed off his tongue like an out-of-control steamroller. "Because I want to get us one – when I'm able to, I mean. I'm doing better at schoolwork now, with Uncle George teaching me, and I'm going to work and save up for a farm – my horse might even win a race for me, and we can all live on it together – just us."

They stopped walking and turned to each other. Devlin was dismayed to see tears running down her cheeks. Then she smiled through them and he realised she wasn't upset. "I think that's a wonderful idea," she told him softly. She took hold of his forearms and whispered, "Devlin, don't ever forget – I love you. I'm sorry for everything we've all been through. Despite everything, I can see you're growing into an awesome young man and I'm proud of you. Remember that, and don't ever give up on your dreams."

Devlin nodded, swallowing a hard lump in his throat. He gave her another hug, more gently this time. "I love you, Mum," his voice croaked into her bony shoulder, "I miss you lots."

"Same, honey." They parted and continued walking, the chattering of the young children taking their attention but not shattering the feeling of closeness between them.

Soon the conversation became more light-hearted as Devlin described the previous morning's attempts at baking and Saraia's rescue mission to help prepare the lovely morning tea ahead of them.

While they were all eating, Devlin held his youngest sister, now awake. He gazed on her wonderingly, amazed at the way her personality was coming through already. She fixed her dark blue eyes on his nose and tried to grab it determinedly, then she pulled his long fringe. "Ouch, little Jade, letting me know who's boss already, eh?" he asked softly, prising the tight fist from his hair.

The visit came to an end too soon, and Devlin found himself watching them all load back into the van. Once again he had a huge lump in his throat.

As they drove away, instead of following George inside, Devlin strode out to see his horse. Zak immediately came to the fence and put his head over. Devlin grasped his arms around the strong neck and buried his face in the blond mane, letting his hiccupping sobs rise to the surface. Zak stood still; strong, warm and calm. Devlin took comfort in his solidness.

Then a firm hand gripped his shoulder from behind. Feeling ashamed, he turned to face Uncle George.

Instead of seeing the scorn he feared, the man's eyes were brimming with tears. He pulled Devlin to his chest in a strong hug and Devlin let the sobs come once more, relieved.

Despite Uncle George's outward gruffness, Devlin realised he had found a man he could trust with his real self. In fact, he suddenly had the feeling that Uncle George had seen him that way right from the beginning.

CHAPTER ELEVEN

"That's it, Devlin, just rest your weight on him at first."

Devlin was lying draped over the horse's bare back while Uncle George held the lead rope. Zak was wearing a riding bridle with neck-length reins. They were using an indoor arena, as Uncle George had explained it was the safest place for Devlin to learn to ride his horse and for the horse to learn to be ridden.

Zak didn't move his legs but turned his head to look curiously at Devlin. He let out a sigh and relaxed. "Good boy," George stroked the horse's face between the eyes. "Okay, now slowly bring your leg up and sit on him, but don't sit straight up yet."

Devlin obeyed. Zak didn't appear to notice any difference.

"Now, slowly straighten up."

Devlin sat up and grinned. At last he was sitting *on* his horse instead of staring at his great hindquarters from the cart.

Zak nuzzled George as if to say, "Okay, this is getting boring, when are we going to *do* something?"

"All right. I'll lead him, you just sit quietly. Don't make any sudden, jerky movements."

As Zak walked forward, Devlin felt him stiffen at the unaccustomed weight on his back, and legs touching his sides. After a round of the arena, the horse had relaxed again, accepting this new feeling.

George made several more rounds until he was certain Zak wasn't going to act upset. Then he unclipped him and allowed Devlin to have control while he still walked in front, encouraging the horse to follow. Eventually George stopped and stood in the middle of the arena. Devlin tried to get Zak to respond to the pressure from his legs. At first the horse looked at George and seemed confused, but then his characteristic obedience came through and he listened to Devlin on his back and walked around the arena, several times in both directions.

George nodded approvingly; horse and boy were a

team once more. It was just a matter of time and practice for both. "That's great, Devlin. You've made good progress. Tomorrow we'll do it all again – and a bit more besides."

"When will I be able to ride him on the farm and through the forest to the beach?" Devlin asked eagerly.

"Not for a while yet," George answered gruffly. When he saw Devlin's face fall, he added, "It'll come soon enough. I'll come with you on the quad bike. Not a good idea for you to go alone, so don't get any bright ideas about that!"

Devlin nodded reluctantly, then cheered up as he thought about the fun it would be.

"So there you are!" Both turned to see Saraia peeking around the doorway. "Saw the horse was out of the paddock and figured you couldn't be *that* far away." She looked at Devlin sitting astride his horse. "Well, whaddaya know? Something the matter with driving him?"

Devlin shook his head, grinning. "I just want to learn both, you know."

"Well, don't forget about the driving, you're my star pupil at the moment."

Devlin laughed. "I thought I was your only pupil."

She shrugged her shoulders, straight-faced and said, "Well, that too."

George interrupted them. "Make sure you dismount as slowly as you got on. We don't want to end a positive session with thoughtless haste."

Devlin's face grew serious again as he paid heed to the instructions. Zak turned his head once more to study what was going on, but showed no concern.

Devlin took the horse's lead from George and rewarded Zak with a rub between the eyes. Then he led the horse away while George and Saraia walked together to the house.

Devlin heard George saying, "Maybe you'd like to come for a quad bike ride, when Devlin and I attempt the forest ..."

Their voices faded, but Devlin could see by the way Saraia was smiling and nodding, she was probably saying yes. He was glad; it would be even more fun if she came too. Maybe he should suggest a picnic. He hoped it wouldn't be too long before they could go.

Two weeks later, Devlin was up to riding Zak in a paddock, with saddle and bridle, walking over poles and doing other confidence-building exercises. The horse was athletic and fit. *He should be,* Devlin thought, *he's working on the track nearly every day and being ridden as well.*

The thing Devlin was most pleased about was Zak's

eyes. They now looked like the other horses on the farm – bright and alert, observing the outer world instead of being drawn into the inner.

Devlin felt everything about his horse was a pleasure. He had grown in confidence to work more with the other horses. Each had their funny ways and personalities, but he felt Zak was a cut above the rest. Safe and reliable, obedient and fun, gentle and yet with so much power to give.

Tomorrow was Saturday, and Devlin wondered if George would decide it was the day for a big ride.

"Monday," was the short and gruff answer when Devlin asked him at afternoon tea time.

"Why Monday?" Devlin asked curiously.

"Too many people around the forest and beach on the weekends. Motorbikes, horses, dogs – too much risk of your horse getting spooked."

"I suppose," Devlin answered. "It's just that he's so quiet, I don't really expect him to spook at anything."

George raised his eyebrows. "You just wait and see, boy. He'll be a different horse the first time you take him into that forest. Don't forget he's been born, raised and trained on nothing but farms and tracks. He'll be looking at things like they've got two heads to begin with."

Devlin laughed. He couldn't imagine Zak acting that

way. "Will Saraia be able to come on Monday?"

George nodded. "I already checked." He was quiet for a moment, then said, "Races tonight."

Devlin nodded. He hadn't expected anything different. They had been attending ever since the night they bought Zak. Devlin enjoyed going. It was fun to watch Saraia bring in the winners. The more he watched the races and listened to everyone around him, the more he learned about the sport of harness racing. Secretly he dreamt of the day he would bring Zak back to the track.

He hadn't heard any more mysterious comments from Allan about suspected 'goings on' but had noticed the man was keeping a written record of his observations. "Best you don't know for now, Devlin," was the only answer he gave when Devlin asked about it.

Sometimes he would see Allan stopping to sit and talk with people. He would take out his pocket Bible and read to them from it. One of those times, Devlin saw a man had tears in his eyes. After talking a good while, Allan handed the man an envelope.

"What was the matter?" Devlin asked Allan later.

"He had just lost the last of his money on a foolish bet. I didn't know, but I stopped to talk about God's love with him and he broke down. He confessed he was considering ending his life, rather than going home to the family he felt he had let down."

"What did you give him?"

"I prayed with him and gave him a grocery voucher, so he could take some food home for his family and try again."

Devlin puzzled over all this for a long time after they returned home from the races that week. He wondered what would make Allan want to go out of his way for a complete stranger.

Sitting in the kitchen after dinner, Devlin had a question for George. "Um … Uncle George?"

"Mmm," the man grunted, his nose in a harness-racing magazine.

"Are you still able to take a horse to the races, if you wanted to?"

He was disappointed to see him shake his head.

"How come?"

"Let my licence lapse."

"Can you get it back?"

George finally raised his eyes to look at him.

"What would I want to do that for?"

Devlin swallowed. "To race Zak for me."

"You been talking to Allan about this?"

Devlin frowned. "No."

George grunted. "Huh. He mentioned the same idea

the other day."

Devlin's face lit up. "Really? He must think the same as me then, that my horse deserves another chance."

"It'll cost me some money."

"To race him?"

"Yeah – and to get my licence back."

"But you might do it?"

George stared at him long and hard then said, "Tell you what – I need to see him do some fast work-outs first. If he doesn't show something there, I needn't take it any further."

"Will I get to drive him?"

George shook his head. "Nope. Saraia can do that for us. If he's gonna be a racehorse again, she'd be his driver anyway. If he doesn't show any new spark, then eventually you'll be able to try him on some fast work-outs yourself, just for the experience."

Devlin let out an elated "Ye-ah!"

George snorted. "You sound like a donkey. Better start thinking about what you're gonna bake for that picnic on Monday, hadn't you? Gotta impress the lady if you want her to drive your racehorse."

Devlin immediately went and grabbed the recipe book from the kitchen shelf. Secretly he wondered if there was more to George's desire to 'impress the lady'. Then he got lost in the world of ingredients and chocolate temptations. It was a pleasant feeling when he realised it was no longer so much trouble to read the pages. The home schooling was really starting to pay off.

Monday dawned with a pink and orange sky in the east. Devlin was up and racing around the early chores before George had stumbled out the front door. He wanted to get breakfast out of the way as early as possible because he knew he had to put in some schoolwork as well before they would be able to set off on the big ride.

Saraia arrived in time for a breakfast of creamy porridge sprinkled with brown sugar, and crumpets dripping with butter, honey and Marmite.

"Gee – you blokes sure eat well," she commented, patting her slim stomach.

"That's because we work well," said George, his eyes twinkling.

Saraia's eyes narrowed. "Insinuating ...?"

George's mouth twitched at the corners. "Well ... the boy here had all the chores done in record time. The cow hardly had time to blink. And where were you?"

She flicked a crumpet crumb off her plate at him. "You know very well I had to drive here from my parents' farm in the Waitakeres." She lost her indignant tone. "I stopped at a supermarket as well. Thought I'd add some goodies to the hamper today." George and Devlin waited for her to explain, but instead she grinned cheekily and said, "And you'll just have to wait and see what!"

Devlin sat comfortably in the saddle astride Zak, who stood patiently, waiting for the command to walk forward. George and Saraia finished packing the quad bike and then they climbed on. The bike rumbled into life and Devlin pressed his horse to follow it. They went into a paddock, which changed from pasture to bush about halfway down the slope. Zak went hesitantly at first, in the habit of either going to the barn, track or the upper paddocks. Then he accepted the new direction and walked jauntily.

When they entered the bush, however, Zak stopped dead and stared about. Devlin got him going again, but after a few more paces the horse stopped again. This happened several times.

He was getting left behind by the quad bike and soon he realised the motor had stopped. They must have paused to wait for him to catch up.

Zak became increasingly tense; stopping, head raised, nostrils quivering, walking a few steps. Suddenly he whipped around to canter back the way he had come.

"Woah!" Devlin only just managed to stop him from bolting. He slowly made the horse turn around. The horse took a few steps forward and Devlin rubbed his neck, encouraging him to continue. "It's okay, fella, there's nothing to worry about."

George walked towards them. He had left the quad behind and come to help. A twig snapped loudly under his foot. Zak jumped and once more tried to whip around. Devlin held him and prevented the flight once more.

George reached the horse's head. He clipped a lead rope on to the halter that the horse was still wearing under his bridle. "Come on mate, we'd better lead you until you get used to this new place – else we'll take all day to get to that lunch spot."

Devlin felt relieved. Zak was more relaxed now that he had a leader in front of him. The three made their way to where Saraia waited with the quad bike. She started the bike up again and rode slowly along in front, following the little-used trail through the bush. Each time they came to a gate, she would open it for the group and close it after them. Soon they came out down near the lake.

Everyone remained silent as they passed by the gravestones. They followed the lake around until they left it once more and entered the tall, quiet forest.

It seemed to Devlin that they had been walking for ages. His rumbling tummy agreed. "Aren't you getting tired of walking, Uncle George?" he asked eventually.

"Yep. Not far now though."

"Will you have to lead him home as well?"

"Don't think so. He'll be feeling familiar with it all by then and happy to be heading back to his paddock. You'll just have to be careful he doesn't get too keen – keep him under control."

Devlin nodded, although he was aware that George wasn't looking at him, but ahead.

The forest floor was becoming very sandy. Suddenly they stepped out of it into bright sunshine and began climbing a sand dune. Zak put his nose down to the sand and snorted. His hooves sunk down but he ploughed on bravely. George had to work to keep ahead of the horse's powerful strides.

Saraia had already reached the top and she sat there, smiling, as she watched them. When they reached the top, Devlin looked around him and sucked in his breath. "Cool!"

The ocean lay directly in front of him, surf pounding in wild, foaming waves, the beach disappearing into the distance, left and right.

"Do you think he'd be okay to have a flat-out gallop, Uncle George?" Devlin asked, eyes bright with anticipation.

"Walk him out and see what he does," George

instructed. He unclipped the lead rope and let Devlin take the horse down the other side of the sand dune and onto the beach.

Zak tossed his head, snorting and breathing the salty air. The crashing of the waves up the beach towards him made him fidget nervously. But Devlin felt the horse was calm enough to keep responding to his commands. He headed him up the beach towards Southhead.

He walked at first then eased into a trot. Then he went into his natural racing gait – pacing. Devlin squeezed his calves, telling the horse he wanted something different.

Eventually Zak cantered and Devlin let him discover the feel of this on the soft sand. Then he loosened his hold enough to let the horse know he could extend as much as he wanted. Zak obliged, uncertainly at first then with reckless abandon. Devlin felt exhilarated. His eyes watered in the wind as the horse galloped hard. The surf crashed on their left. Devlin let the horse run his heart out and didn't ask him to stop until he felt him tiring and slowing of his own accord. When they finally dropped down to a walk, Devlin turned Zak in a large semicircle and looked back the way they had come. George, Saraia and the quad were just faint specks.

"Man, you sure can run when you want to, can't you, boy?" Devlin whispered. He leaned forward and patted

Zak's sweating neck.

Now that they were facing the way home, Devlin could feel Zak quickening again, asking to run once more. "Okay, boy!" Devlin let out a whoop of delight as they built up into a fast gallop. He felt wild, happy and free.

Zak's maximum pace didn't last as long this time, but he easily maintained a steady canter. Devlin had a feeling he should pull him up to a walk, well before he reached George and Saraia, just in case the horse decided to give the lunch break a miss and head straight for home.

Ever the well-mannered horse, Zak responded to Devlin and slowed to a walk and they approached the quad bike. Zak's nostrils were flared and he was covered in sand and sweat. He was breathing hard but not distressed.

George gave Devlin a curt nod.

"How was it?" Saraia asked, grinning from ear to ear.

"It was wicked!" Devlin burst out.

"It looked like fun," Saraia said, "I wouldn't mind going for a blat like that, myself."

George eyed the sweating, blowing horse. "Didn't do him any harm, either, a good blowout like that. His eyes look brighter than ever. Keep him walking though, till his heart rate comes down a bit more."

"I'll take him over to the water, see what he does,"

Devlin said, turning the horse away again.

"We'll get lunch ready," Saraia called out.

Devlin took Zak down to the ocean. The first time the horse stood in the shallow water, he put his head down to it and snorted, smelling the salty foam and seaweed flowing around his hooves. He curled his top lip, looking comical. Devlin laughed.

Then a breaker crashed down, too close for comfort, and Zak jumped sideways. Devlin nearly came unseated but quickly righted himself. He walked Zak up and down in the water, up to the horse's knees, until he felt the horse was used to this new sport.

Then he remembered lunch. He could see plastic cups filled with cola and juice, sitting on the bike. He suddenly felt parched. When he reached the bike, Devlin dismounted and loosened Zak's girth slightly.

George had tied a piece of baling twine to the back of the quad and he now clipped the horse lead onto Zak and secured him with a safety release knot to the baling twine. "So we lose the baling twine first, not the bike, the gear, or the horse," George reminded Devlin.

Saraia produced an ice-cream container full of fresh water and offered Zak a small drink. He slurped half the container in one suck. "Better save the rest," she told him, putting the lid back on and tucking it back into the picnic basket.

"Now ..." Saraia spread her goodies out on the bike seat. "We have chocolate mud cake, chicken-filled rolls, and banana muffins. Okay?"

"Mmm ..." Devlin and George made approving noises as they made their selection.

"I made scones filled with jam and whipped cream," Devlin said through a mouthful of mud cake. "They should be in a container there somewhere."

"I brought sandwiches: egg, luncheon, cheese-marmite-and-lettuce," George stated. "Oh – and the drinks and a chocolate bar each, for the journey home."

"Cool picnic!" Devlin said to nobody in particular. "Any more drink?"

Saraia plucked a large bottle out of the basket and refilled his cup. "I agree, it's good to get out and do something different and fun like this—hey!"

Devlin turned just in time to see the horse devouring a sandwich and stretching out to reach the mud cake. He laughed and gently backed Zak away from the food. When George and Saraia weren't looking, he gave him his bread crusts. "I'll bring an apple or carrot or something, next time, boy," he whispered apologetically, patting the horse's long chestnut nose.

Zak snorted and began to paw the sand with his

hoof. Devlin watched him, ignorant of what it meant. Then, suddenly, the horse acted as though he was about to lie down!

"Whatcha doing?" Devlin said, suddenly panicking.

George turned, saw what was happening and quickly removed the horse's saddle and blanket. He released the lead rope from the baling twine and handed the end of it to Devlin. "You hold the lead. Keep it loose but out of his way. Just watch, it'll be okay. He wants a treat."

Devlin stood there and watched, chuckling, as Zak dropped down onto the sand and began to roll. He grunted with pleasure, rolling right over.

Saraia counted the rolls. "One hundred, two hundred, three hundred, four hundred!"

"What are you counting for?" asked Devlin.

She laughed. "It's an old saying I heard a long time ago. Count the rolls and that's how much the horse is worth!"

Devlin grinned. "Better make his rolls a hundred *thousand* each. That's at least how much I need him to win me at the races!"

Saraia raised her eyebrows at George. "Races?"

George shrugged his shoulders. "We'll see."

CHAPTER TWELVE

The ride back to the farm was peaceful and uneventful. Zak was alert to the bush surroundings but no longer bothered by them. Devlin felt happy. The beach gallop had been awesome and he hoped he would be able to do it again soon.

Once the bike had been put away and Zak washed down, dried, covered and put in his paddock, they went inside. George checked for phone messages and found an urgent one to ring Aroha.

Devlin watched as George phoned Aroha. His curiosity turned to alarm as the man turned pale. "I – I'll put Devlin on." His tone was grave. "You'll come out to see him? All right. Good."

"What? What is it?" Devlin felt panic rising and tightening to a knot in his chest. George didn't answer but looked pale and shocked, holding out the phone.

Devlin put the phone to his ear, dread sweeping over him like a black cloud. "Hi, Aroha? What's wrong?"

"Devlin – is George with you?" Her voice cracked as if it were breaking.

Devlin felt George slip his arm around his waist. Saraia stood on the other side and did the same thing.

"Yes.... why? What's happened?"

"It's your mother, Devlin. She was taken to the emergency ward at the hospital late last night. There was a lot of confusion. They didn't know who she was at first. She had been badly beaten up, and had no ID on her. Her boyfriend came in with her. He'd driven her in but was drunk on his feet. He passed out and it wasn't until they could get some information out of him early this morning, that they found out who she was."

"What about the kids? Where are they?" Devlin was finding it hard to breathe.

"Right now, they're in emergency foster care. A neighbour heard some commotion and found the children home alone, so she stayed with them. When your mother hadn't come home by morning, she rang the police."

He dreaded the next response. "Is my mum – is she –

is she gonna be okay?" He felt sick to his stomach as he waited for the answer.

Aroha was silent for a moment, her breathing was shaky and Devlin realised she was crying. "She didn't make it, hon." Her voice was a hoarse, shaky whisper. "I'm so sorry."

As the shocking words hit him, he sagged against the arms around his waist.

He began to sob. "Was it him? Was it that scumbag boyfriend of hers who did it? Did he kill my mum?"

Aroha choked. "The police arrested him today, Devlin. In his drunken state he'd already confessed to the hospital staff that he'd lost it and not meant to go so far."

"I hope he rots–" Devlin's voice broke as he dropped his head and shoulders, shaking with sobs. "I hate him! I hate him! Oh, Mum … Mu-um …" He dropped the phone.

George turned him around and hugged him. Devlin tried to beat him with his fists, sobs muffled as his face pressed against the man's chest.

Saraia picked up the phone and spoke quietly to Aroha while George continued to hold Devlin, letting him pour out his grief and anguish. George's chin quivered, as he remembered – as if it were yesterday – beating the same type of grief on the ground of a steep ravine.

Devlin was on the practice track, jogging Zak, doing their regular work-out. He wiped away tears with the back of his hand. It had been three weeks, but every work-out had been the same – his chance to cry in private.

Aroha had come to visit him the day after the terrible news. She brought the three older children with her, leaving Jade with her caregivers. Solemn and wide-eyed, they had all clung to Devlin, seeking comfort in his familiarity. In return he held them close and whispered to each, "I love you." He did not know how else to comfort them, or himself.

Aroha told him the two boys were staying with Aunty Rose, and Tracy and baby Jade were staying with another couple that Devlin had never met.

"I'd like you to come and spend a weekend at each home, Devlin," Aroha told him. "The children need to keep a sense of family bond with you." Devlin understood – he was all they had now.

He urged Zak a little faster, as he thought back on the funeral, simple and plain as it had been. His mother hadn't reached out to many for friendship, nor did she have any close relations who were interested in, or able to come to, her funeral. Devlin had sat through it, supported by George, Aroha and Rose. He had hardly been able to breathe, thanks to the hard lump in his throat.

His three younger siblings all sat beside him, struggling to understand why Mummy wasn't with them anymore. Baby Jade sat in Rose's arms, gurgling and happy. Devlin couldn't help but feel amazed at the joy and hope a baby could bring to people, even in the midst of such deep pain. He swung between feeling guilty about it and feeling comforted.

A snort behind him broke into his thoughts. A quick glance back and he saw that Allan had come onto the track with Betty. He eased back on the reins a bit, slowing his horse down so that Allan could draw alongside.

"How are ya, mate?" Allan asked kindly.

Devlin nodded in reply. He couldn't trust himself to speak about his feelings, still raw every time he remembered his mother was gone.

"He's looking good, ain't he?" Allan was looking at Zak, admiring his muscled physique.

Devlin managed a small smile. "Yep."

"Hey, Devlin, uh … I wanted to talk to you about something …" Allan hesitated.

"Yeah?"

"I don't know whether you've picked up on it, but

uh ... George and Saraia seem to be getting along real good. Sort of forming a close friendship – you know what I mean?"

"You mean like they're a couple?" Devlin asked.

Allan nodded. "Yeah – sort of like dating, only they just hang out, spending time together."

Devlin thought about it. Saraia had been visiting a lot. He had thought more than once it might be becoming more than just an 'old mates' friendship. "I s'pose," he answered eventually.

"Just thought I'd mention it. I mean, you've had a lot on your mind, and I wanted to make sure you were prepared for any possible changes ahead, whatever they may be."

Devlin nodded again. "Thanks."

He finished his work-out before Allan, so found himself alone at the tie-up area when Saraia drove up in her hatchback. She got out and walked casually over to give Zak a pat. "Hiya, Devlin."

"Hi, Saraia."

"Hey, can I ask for your opinion on something?"

"Yep." Devlin was glad he'd talked with Allan, once he heard her next words.

"I guess you've noticed that me and George, well, we sort of have feelings for each other. You know – girlfriend-boyfriend stuff. Are you okay with that?"

Devlin nodded.

"Cool," she smiled, looking relieved. "It feels a bit weird because I was friends with his late wife, Helen. Now that she's not here and this is happening, I can't help but wonder how she'd feel about it, you know?"

Devlin nodded, then suggested shyly, "If Helen loved George, she wouldn't mind him having happiness in the rest of his life. It doesn't change what they had in the past. She liked you, so I bet she'd be glad he's got someone nice."

Saraia wiped tears from her eyes. She reached out and gave Devlin a hug. "You're the best, Devlin. Thank you."

As she walked away to find George in the house, Devlin thought she looked as if a weight had lifted from her shoulders. He couldn't help but think about his words and how they might apply to his mum. "What would you want for me now, Mum?" he whispered. Then he remembered her last visit and how she had encouraged him not to give up on his dreams.

He finished getting Zak ready to go back out to his paddock then stood, deep in thought, stroking the horse's long nose.

"We've got a challenge ahead of us, big boy," Devlin told the horse quietly. "But we're gonna go for it, no matter what. But first of all I need to talk to Uncle George again about letting you race."

Back in his paddock, Zak snorted with pleasure as he put his head down to the grass. Devlin shut the gate then headed straight to the house. The door was open and, as he began to remove his boots, Saraia's voice floated out to him. "But what about Devlin? He can't stay here after the wedding ..."

George's reply was gruff. "I'll speak to Aroha about it. She'll have to find him somewhere."

Devlin froze. His hands began to shake. He felt as if he had been kicked solidly in the stomach.

Saraia again, "I doubt he'll be very happy about it. He won't be able to take his horse."

George, "Can't be helped ..."

Devlin had heard enough. He slipped his boots back on and ran to the gear shed. His heart and mind were in turmoil. All the trust he had built up in George and staying at this farm, hoping it was home, lay shattered like broken glass in the pit of his stomach. The old Devlin, angry, rebellious, rejected, rose up inside of him like never before. He seized Zak's riding bridle and ran out to the paddock. He caught Zak, removed his cover, slid on the bridle and mounted him bareback off the gate. Allan, coming off the track with Betty, called out to him.

Devlin refused to turn towards him. *Is that what you were warning me about, Allan? The possible changes ahead? You knew!*

Devlin pushed his horse into a trot and headed to the bush path that they had followed on the day of the picnic. He rode as hard as the terrain would allow, stopping to open gates, leaving them open behind him, not caring if he let stock out of the paddocks.

Once he was by the lake there were no more gates so he recklessly pushed Zak into a hard run, entering the forest at breakneck speed. He wanted to get to the beach where they could just run and run. He had no logical thoughts of what he would do after that, all he could think about was getting away, outrunning the painful feelings of betrayal.

The next thing he heard was the revving of a motorbike crossing his path and, before he had time to react, his horse and the bike were heading for a collision. He tried to pull Zak to the right, giving the bike time to get across in front of them. Zak tried to leap over the rear tyre but landed awkwardly and stumbled sideways. Devlin shot over the horse's right shoulder. Everything went black.

When Devlin came to, his body screamed with pain. It was dark and his hearing was fuzzy. He tried to figure out what he was lying on, but felt tired and slipped back into oblivion. This happened over and over again. He couldn't move. Sometimes he thought he could hear voices, far away, but once more the tiredness would overtake him and he would fade out again.

The next time he woke he could hear a droning, buzzing sound. He struggled to hear it better and recognised it as a male voice, talking near his ear. Sleep tried to take him again but he fought desperately. Suddenly it was as if his ears popped and the fuzziness partially went. The voice became clearer and sharper. It sounded like Allan. After a time, Devlin realised the man was quietly praying.

Slowly, a heaviness lifted off Devlin's body and he felt hot all over. He opened his eyes and stared upwards … at the ceiling of a hospital room. He turned his head and stared at Allan. The man had his head bowed. His lips were still murmuring in quiet prayer.

When Devlin opened his mouth to speak, he found he was hoarse and could barely make a sound. He pushed himself harder. "You can stop bothering Him now," he croaked out.

Allan raised his eyes, his face puffy with concern and fatigue. But now it lit up like a thousand candles. "Devlin!"

Then he laughed. "It's no bother, believe me! But don't try to talk yet, I'll get the nurse." He pushed a buzzer and moments later a nurse entered the room.

"Problem?" she asked briskly.

"Nope – just the opposite," Allan nodded towards Devlin, whose eyelids were getting heavy again.

"Wonderful! I'll get the doctor."

Devlin slipped back into a doze.

The next time he woke, he found George and Saraia sitting watching him.

His first thoughts were for his horse. "Zak – how is he? Was he ... ?"

"He's fine," Saraia smiled reassuringly. "He saved your life, you know."

"I don't remember anything except the motorbike ... then Zak jumping and stumbling."

"That horse is your friend, all right," said George. "And the lad on the bike knew not to move you. He covered you with his jacket, which was all he had. Then he slapped the horse on the rump, hoping he would run home and alert someone that you needed help."

"Which is exactly what he did," Saraia continued. "He galloped back towards the house and met us on the quad, coming to find you. Allan told us you had taken off, acting really weird. As soon as Zak saw us, he about-turned again and led us to where you were. I called for the emergency chopper to come and pick you up."

"You've got a head injury and broken ribs, the doctors told us," George added. "If the chopper hadn't got to you when it did, the results could have been much worse. You were losing a lot of blood from that head wound. Collided with a tree, the bikie said."

Suddenly, Devlin remembered he was furious with Uncle George and Saraia and frowned at them. "Anyway, what are you doing here?"

George looked startled. "What do ya mean, what am I doing here? Where else would I be?"

Devlin looked away. "Making plans for your future. Without me."

Saraia spoke up gently. "I don't know what you mean, Devlin. All of George's future includes you."

"That's not what I heard."

George sounded indignant. "I wasn't going to ask you straight away what made you take off in such a darn hurry, but you'd better explain. What did you hear?"

Devlin took a deep, angry breath. When he spoke his voice came out tense and hard. "I trusted you, Uncle George. You are the first man I have ever trusted. I hoped you wanted me to stay, that you wouldn't send me away. But then, I heard you and Saraia talking. When you get married, you don't want me to live with you anymore." He was breathing hard with distress and his ribs hurt.

"Oh, for goodness sake, Devlin, you heard *so* wrong!" Saraia exclaimed with indignant horror. "All we were talking about is when we get married and go away for a couple of weeks holiday, we won't be able to leave you by yourself at the farm!"

George nodded. "That's right. I've talked to Aroha about it and she agrees it would be a good opportunity for you to have a visit with your brothers and sisters. Stay one week with Tracy and Jade and the other week with Zachary and Sammy."

Saraia butted in. "We know you'll miss your horse and everything, but it'll only be for a couple of weeks. George'll get someone to mind the farm while we're away."

Devlin stared at them both in disbelief. "You sure that's all you were saying?"

George leaned towards him and said quietly, a smile playing at the corners of his mouth. "I've applied for my trainer's licence. Do you think I did that for nothing? I doubt that horse'd win a race without you there to look after him."

Devlin groaned, feeling foolish. "I am so stupid."

George glared at him. "No. I can understand, considering your background, why you thought what you did.

Just do me a favour, okay?"

Devlin squinted at him. "What?"

"Next time you *think* you've heard me say something you don't like, have it out with me – face to face. No running away!"

Devlin grinned sheepishly.

Saraia grinned. "So, you'll just have to hurry up and get better. There's so much to organise, what with the wedding and finding out if Zak will race again. Nothing's going to happen without you, we'll just take turns at working him until you're home again."

Devlin nodded, feeling exhausted. He drifted off to sleep with the words '*home again*' dancing at the forefront of his mind. They collided with clouds of uncertainty. His deep craving to belong still felt unfulfilled.

CHAPTER THIRTEEN

"Young fellas usually bounce back quickly," the doctor said several days later. He was smiling at Devlin. "A bit tougher for us older folk. You'll be ready to go, I expect, before this week is out."

Devlin let out a whoop, then tried to cover up a wince. His ribs still felt tender, but he didn't want to give the doctor any reason to change his mind. He felt more than ready to go back to the farm.

At last he was in Saraia's hatchback and she was driving him home. "I can't wait to see Zak … and all the other animals too," he told her.

"You'll get a warm greeting from all, I'm sure," Saraia laughed. "I'll be especially glad to see Zak's reaction. He's been a bit listless since you haven't been there. It's nice to have a bond like that with a horse."

"Do you have a special horse, Saraia?"

"I think they're all special, but I do have an old brood mare who holds a secret place in my heart. A long time ago I rescued her from a trainer who was real 'old school', using handling methods I didn't agree with. It's hard for some people to change with the times, you know? There's a lot more knowledge about gentle horse-handling out there these days, if people are open to learning it. This fellow didn't want to know about any new methods. In the end he couldn't work with her and he let me have her for nothing.

"It took time and patience, but she learned to trust me in the end. She's no flash looker, not like your boy, and she's got a big scar on her nose from when she was mistreated, but I love her anyway, you know?"

Devlin nodded. "Yep."

He relaxed in his seat, content to watch the scenery until they turned into the driveway and pulled up in front of the house.

Then Devlin leapt out and ran to Zak's paddock.

"Hey, big boy!"

The horse jerked his head up from grazing and stared at him for a moment. Then he gave a warm, welcoming whinny and walked smartly to the fence.

Devlin rubbed the horse's face. "Hey, boy, I'm back. Thanks for taking care of me that day. Hey, guess what? You're gonna get to race again! But this time, I bet you're gonna show everyone what you can *really* do." Then his voice saddened. "But first, I'm going to have to go away again. Just for a couple of weeks. Then I'll be back and we'll get right into it."

Zak snorted and nuzzled Devlin's shirt. He grinned.

"Hey, Devlin!" Saraia called out the lounge window, "Can you come in here a minute please, so's we can pick a suit for you to wear?"

Devlin's face fell. *A what?* He gave Zak a final pat and said reluctantly, "Gotta go, mate. I'll be back at feed time."

The day of the wedding dawned overcast and drizzly. George and Devlin rushed around doing the early chores, then they both set about getting showered and dressed for the wedding.

Allan and his wife Jackie arrived, dressed in their best.

They had offered to care for the farm while George and Saraia went on their honeymoon. Devlin had never met Jackie but found she was gentle and quietly spoken. The same kind of inner strength and wisdom he saw in Allan shone out of her blue-grey eyes. He liked her a lot.

The night before, George and Devlin had written down lists of everything the farm-sitting couple would need to know. George gave them the spare key for the house and made doubly sure they knew and understood everything that was required.

"Yes, yes, we'll be fine!" the smiling couple assured him. "Come on, it's time to go."

"Yeah, come on, Uncle George," Devlin groaned. "I'm already feeling stuffy in this suit. I can't wait to get it off!"

"All right, all right," George grumped in reply. "Let's get going."

The four of them rushed out the door and jumped into George's four-wheel drive. "Got everything?" Devlin asked.

"I've got the best man and his wife, the groaning groomsman, suitcase in the back. What else is there?" George grumped. Then his eyebrows shot up in horror. "The rings!" He leaped out of the vehicle and rushed back into the house. He reappeared a few minutes later, looking sheepish. "They were already in my pocket."

The ceremony was to be held nearby at Saraia's friend's property, which had a fantastic garden, usually open to the public by appointment only.

Rich autumn yellow, gold and red tree leaves provided a beautiful backdrop to more unusual colours and flowers growing underneath them.

George parked the vehicle and gave Allan the keys, telling him not to leave before George had removed his suitcase and put it in the 'getaway' car. George then met with the celebrant and helped set up the registry table. The spot where the wedding was to take place was in a clearing beside a small lake. In the centre of the lake was a fountain surrounded by delicate water lilies drifting on the surface. Around the clearing were masses of warm-coloured flowerbeds. In another clearing was a large white marquee, where caterers were setting up for the reception.

Guests began to arrive. George hadn't asked a lot of people, but the wedding was a big thing for Saraia and her parents, so a lot of people George and Devlin had never met before were piling out of their cars. Someone even pulled up in a motor home.

Devlin saw Aroha arrive and gave her a wave. She would be taking him to Aunty Rose's house after the wedding reception. He was beginning to get fidgety and felt relieved when finally someone said, "Shhh … here she comes!"

He and George turned to look up the driveway. Devlin expected to see a nice car but instead he saw a horse-drawn carriage, decorated with ribbons and jangling wedding bells, plodding steadily towards the waiting crowd. The driver halted the pair of horses right in front of the people, who moved aside to form an aisle.

The horses shone from immaculate grooming. One of them had a large scar on its nose, and Devlin guessed she was Saraia's special horse.

Saraia's father, a tall, athletic man, hopped down from the carriage and held out his hand to the hidden beauty inside. She took his arm and stepped down gracefully, smiling from ear to ear.

Devlin heard George suck in his breath. Saraia looked beautiful in her white satin dress. The heart-shaped neckline and the bottom hem sparkled with tiny diamante horseshoes. Her hair had been arranged in a fancy style, piled high on her head, with a sparkly horseshoe tiara and a veil flowing behind.

Devlin felt pleased to see such happiness and expectation in her face as she looked towards George, and when Devlin glanced at George he could see nothing but love glowing in his eyes.

Devlin gave a small sigh. *Let the wedding begin!*

The ceremony was short but meaningful and soon it was announced that the couple were husband and wife. Time was spent having photos taken in the gardens, then everyone tucked into a delicious lunch. Devlin enjoyed being part of the wedding party, being served by the caterers and eating as much as he liked.

The wedding gifts covered a large table and Devlin watched as Saraia unwrapped them. Suddenly she turned to him and said, "There's one here with your name on it, Devlin!"

Startled, he stared at the large parcel.

"Well – come on, I'm dying to see what it is!" she laughed.

Devlin carefully unwrapped it and grinned from ear to ear. "A PlayStation!" He glanced around for Allan and Uncle George and spotted them watching him, smiling. "Awesome! Thank you!"

"Just leave it here with the other gifts and it can go with them back home," Saraia told him. "Allan and Jackie will take care of it." She raised her eyebrows cheekily. "I'd quite like a go on that, myself. I hope you're willing to share! We'll have to buy some games."

Devlin laughed and nodded.

The time seemed to fly by and then Saraia reappeared

in a simple blue dress and she and George said their goodbyes.

The horse-drawn carriage had long gone, and the newlyweds surprised everyone by running to the motor home and climbing in. "We're off for a scenic trip!" Saraia called out.

Allan was standing beside Devlin.

"Did you put in Uncle George's suitcase?"

Allan gasped. "Oh no! Don't let them drive off yet!" He rushed off to the four-wheel drive.

Devlin ran over and banged on Saraia's passenger window. She wound it down. "Suitcase, Uncle George!" Devlin panted.

"Here it is!" Allan ran up, carrying the forgotten case.

George got out, placed it in the living area of the motor home, gave Allan and Devlin a bear hug and chuckled. "Thanks."

Devlin watched them go off down the drive, slightly envious of the adventure and fun ahead of them. Then Aroha was by his side, smiling, reminding him of some little children who were looking forward to having him come and stay.

"Awesome!" he exclaimed, "At last I get to take this suit off."

Zachary and Sammy had their noses pressed to the living room window when Aroha pulled up outside. Devlin grinned and gave them a thumbs-up.

As soon as he was in the door the little boys were jumping around his legs, clinging to his jeans and talking excitedly at the same time.

"Aunty Rose has made play dough ..."

"I've got a new truck!"

"Will you play play dough with me, Devwin?"

"Wanna see my truck?"

"Whoah, slow down, little bros. Yes, Sammy, I'll do play dough and yep – let's have a look at your truck, Zachary." Devlin laughed and ruffled each boy's hair playfully.

Their eyes lit up as each one departed on his individual mission. Rose seized the moment to give Devlin a hug.

"So ... how's it going then, Devlin? How was the wedding?"

"Things are going good, Aunty Rose. The wedding was good too."

"I heard you had a nasty accident – came off a horse or something?"

Devlin touched the spot on the top of his head. His hair was now covering the scar. "Yeah ... wasn't the horse's fault. He had to avoid a motorbike and I collided with a tree."

"Goodness! Well, I'm looking forward to hearing about your adventures. We've got a whole week. Uncle Jack is away on a business trip and Helena went with him, so it's just me and the boys – and you, of course." She turned to Aroha. "Like a coffee or tea?"

Aroha smiled apologetically. "I'd love to, but I'm afraid it'll have to be next time. I've got another appointment I need to get to. Are you okay now, Devlin? Sorry I have to rush off."

Devlin nodded. "Yep, that's cool. Thanks a lot for bringing me."

"You're welcome. I'll see you again next weekend, when it's time to visit the girls."

Devlin looked hesitant for a moment, then said, "I'm looking forward to seeing them … but I don't know their caregivers. You sure they don't mind me coming?"

"They don't mind at all." Aroha replied. Then her voice softened. "In fact, they're hoping you might be able to help them with Tracy. She's been a bit withdrawn, you know, since she lost her mum."

Devlin's face saddened at the thought of his little sister being unhappy. He nodded.

"Anyway," Aroha gave him a quick hug, "you enjoy these little boys and I'll see you soon."

The week with his brothers flew past before Devlin even had time to think about it. They kept him so busy that he would crash exhausted into bed at night and fall straight to sleep. They visited the local playground nearly every day, played rough and tussle on the lawn, and kicked a ball around the yard.

"It's like having a rest, with you here," Rose laughingly told Devlin one evening after the little boys had been put to bed. "You keep them so occupied, I hardly have to do anything. At night they're totally worn out and fall asleep like little angels."

Devlin grinned. "Yeah, I miss them heaps when I'm not with them. It feels good to be making up some of the time, even if ..." His voice trailed off and he left his sentence unfinished.

Rose nodded. "Even if not all of your family is here," she finished for him. "The boys miss you too. I'm not looking forward to the sad faces when it's time for you to leave."

Devlin burst out with his feelings. "You know, that's the hardest part. It always has been. I hate it more than anything in the world." He nearly choked on his next words. "The tearing apart of what is supposed to be together."

Rose said quietly, "A lot of kids take their families for granted."

"Well, I never will," Devlin said emphatically.

"Then you might not know it yet," said Rose slowly, "but that is something good that has come out of the bad." She stood up and began preparing a supper of hot chocolate and home-baked biscuits.

Devlin watched, feeling overwhelmed with gratitude for caring people like her.

"So, what did you mean when you said that Tracy's withdrawn?" Devlin asked Aroha as they drove into an unfamiliar Auckland suburb. The lump in his throat had just begun to ease, after a tearful departure from his brothers.

"She hardly speaks to anyone," Aroha explained. "She shows little interest in Jade, sometimes even seems hostile towards her. She won't play with other children. It's like there's a wall between her and everybody. She won't open herself up to bond with her caregivers. It's as if she's retreated into a world all of her own. I don't know how she'll cope when she starts school next term."

"Has anyone tried talking to her, about Mum and stuff?" Devlin asked, a worried frown on his face. He hated the thought of his little sister so upset and lonely.

"Yes, I've tried. Her caregivers have tried. She's seeing

a counsellor as well, but it's very slow progress. It will be good for her to have you back, even if it's just for this week."

Devlin nodded. "I don't know what I can do, except maybe give her lots of cuddles. That's if she'll let me," he added.

"Just take your time," Aroha advised. "Don't push her too hard, but don't be afraid to reach out to her either, if your gut feeling is telling you to."

They pulled up to a grand, two-storey house. "Wow, this is flash," Devlin muttered. "They got any other kids?"

"Three children, all grown up and left home, plus grandchildren. The husband – Mr Smithsfield, or you can call him Uncle Paul – is a lawyer. He's recently cut back on his hours so that he can spend more time with the girls. His wife, Aunty Ange, stays home full-time, of course, to care for them."

Devlin felt a little nervous. Then the longing to see his sisters overcame his hesitation and he walked boldly up the front steps, carrying his bag. He rang the doorbell with Aroha standing beside him.

Sharp, high-pitched barking sounded and the pitter-pattering of a little dog. This was followed by thumping footsteps and Uncle Paul opened the door. "Get down, Spot!" he ordered the little black and white fox terrier, who was jumping up at Devlin's legs. "Hi, Aroha," he smiled. Then he turned to Devlin, holding out his hand to shake. "You must be Devlin. Good to meet you. Come on in. Spot'll settle down in a minute."

Devlin shook his hand and followed the man inside to a large foyer. "Just put your bag here," Paul instructed, "we'll take it to your room soon. Angela is just changing Jade. We'll go upstairs to the living room and you can see them."

"Where's Tracy?" Devlin asked.

"Looking at some books up there. Come on."

Devlin and Aroha followed him up a spiral staircase to the next floor and through a child-safe gate at the top.

They entered a large but cosy lounge. It had plenty of toys for Tracy to enjoy and a large bookshelf, filled with children's books. That was where she was, sitting on a bean chair, looking at the pages of a book.

"Hey, Trace," Devlin exclaimed, walking towards her. He was suddenly struck by her likeness to his mother.

She looked up and stared. She appeared thin and unhappy. Her eyes were dull at first, then a glow of recognition brightened them.

Devlin went down on one knee in front of her and held his arms open, asking for a hug. "Hey, lil sis! I've missed you! Can I have a hug?"

Slowly she put the book down and stood up, uncertain. Then she surged forward, into his arms, pressing herself against his chest. He held her firmly but gently and kissed the side of her head. He was glad he had his back to the watching adults as his tears fell into Tracy's hair.

They stayed that way for a long time. Devlin's legs began to cramp, but he was determined he wouldn't be the first to break the embrace. Finally, she moved to take a step back and she stared into his face again.

"Is Mummy coming back too?" she whispered, hazel eyes wide and hopeful.

Devlin took each of her hands in his. "No, sweetie," he whispered, watching her face. "Mummy's gone now. She can't be with us anymore."

The pale face crumpled. "But I *want* her!"

Devlin gently pulled her into another hug, tears stinging his eyes. "So do I, Trace. But you know what? At least we've still got each other. I've come to stay with you for a little while, did you know that?"

She nodded. "Please don't go away again."

Devlin could only squeeze his eyes shut as he held her. He hoped that when the time came for him to leave, she would be strong enough to handle it.

"This is a real big house! Gonna show me around?" he asked, taking one of her hands.

She nodded and led him towards the kitchen.

Devlin spotted Jade lying happily under a baby play gym. He nodded in greeting to the slim, dark-haired woman who was kneeling beside her. She smiled warmly. "Nice to meet you at last, Devlin. I'm Aunty Ange. Just make yourself at home, okay?"

"Okay, thanks," Devlin replied. "Tracy is showing me around."

"Wonderful!" Devlin saw Aunty Ange wipe a tear from her eye. "Just wonderful."

Devlin had just as much fun in his week with Tracy and Jade as he had with the boys. Tracy's spirits picked up quickly, and Devlin was able to have some good talks with her about her thoughts and feelings.

"I don't like Jade," she told him, when he was giving the baby a cuddle and feeding her a bottle.

"How come?" he asked, keeping his tone relaxed.

Her hazel eyes filled with tears. "Coz it's her fault Mummy left us."

"Why do you think that?"

"I dunno," she looked down at the carpet, fiddling with a small doll in her hand. "Coz she cried lots and Mummy got tired."

"No, that's not what happened."

Her face turned up to him, frightened. "Whose fault was it?" she whispered.

"Tracy, it wasn't your fault . . . or Jade's . . . or Zachary's or Sammy's or mine. So don't think like that any more, okay? You need to love Jade and help take care of her. You're her big sister and she needs you to love her, just like I love you both."

She stared uncertainly at Jade.

"Okay?"

Tracy nodded, her face sombre. "Can I feed her too?"

Devlin smiled. "Yeah! Hop up beside me."

She sat propped up against the cushions and Devlin placed the guzzling Jade across her lap, head supported by her arm. "I'll sit beside you and if she gets too heavy, you let me know, okay?"

Tracy smiled, the first real grin Devlin had seen since he arrived. "Drink up, Jade," she ordered her sister importantly. It was Devlin's turn to grin. The old, confident, bossy Tracy was coming back.

By the time the week came to an end, Tracy was looking happier. She was talking more to her caregivers and being protective towards Jade instead of hostile.

On his last night with her, Devlin read Tracy a bedtime story. She snuggled down in bed, hugged her teddy and listened. When he finished, he said, "You know I'm leaving tomorrow morning, eh Tracy?"

She nodded and her chin quivered. "Where you gonna go?" she asked.

"I'm still living at the farm. You remember visiting me there? I showed you my horse, Zak."

She nodded. "Why can't you live here?"

"Coz my home is Uncle George's farm. I'm doing really well there and I've got the horse to look after. You're gonna do real well living here too."

"Will you come back?"

Devlin nodded. "'Course I will! As soon as I can, okay? It might just be for a weekend or something … and hopefully you'll be able to visit me at the farm again."

"And Jade?"

"Yep, Jade too." He kissed her on the forehead. "G'night Trace, love ya."

"Nigh-night." She reached up and gripped him around the back of his neck, holding him down. Grinning, he gently removed her arms and slipped from the room.

CHAPTER FOURTEEN

The next day's departure went better than he expected. Tracy seemed to be feeling a lot more secure and settled within herself since Devlin had helped answer some of her questions. She stood in the driveway, holding Aunty Ange's hand and waving at him with her free one. He waved back, smiling. "See you again soon!" he called out the window.

"Bye!" he heard her voice faintly before he wound the window back up.

Alec, a male social worker, was driving him back to the farm as Aroha was away on leave.

"Everything cool, bro?" Alec asked. He was tall, well-built and dark-skinned, with short, neatly cropped hair.

"Yeah, my little sisters are awesome," Devlin replied.

"Tracy looks like one choice little girl," Alec answered. "She thinks you're pretty cool too, eh?"

Devlin grinned. "Yeah." Then he became pensive as his thoughts turned towards Uncle George, Saraia and the farm.

As if reading his mind, Alec asked, "Looking forward to going home?"

"Yeah, just wondering if things are going to be much different," Devlin answered, "Uncle George just got married."

"Mmm … some things might be, eh? What do you think?" Alec asked.

Devlin thought for a moment, then said, "Saraia's a real good cook – so that'll be good."

"Yep, what else?" Alec asked.

"Uncle George might not have as much time for me, because he'll be spending it with her."

"Sort of like having a Mum and Dad, eh?" Alec suggested.

"Yeah … I guess. I've never had a proper Mum-and-Dad-type home."

"Maybe you could sit down and have a talk with them," said Alec. "You could ask them what time they want for themselves and when they can give time to you.

Just so's you all know where you stand. You know what I'm saying, bro?"

Devlin nodded. "Yeah – Uncle George said he wants me to talk with him about stuff, face to face, rather than run away."

"Sounds like a plan." Alec smiled.

They were quiet for a while, then Devlin said, "Can't wait to see my horse."

"You got your own horse, bro?"

"Yeah – he's a racehorse – a standardbred."

"So he has a jockey and goes to the races?"

"Nah, the thoroughbreds are the gallopers – they get ridden. My horse is a pacer – pulls the driver in a sulky."

Devlin chatted to Alec the rest of the way to the farm, telling him all about Zak and his hopes to race him soon.

As they pulled up in front of the house, Alec said, "I'd better come and meet your racehorse then, eh bro?"

"Cool," Devlin said.

They got out of the car and Devlin led the way to Zak's paddock. The horse raised his head, recognised Devlin and gave a welcoming whinny. He came over to the fence and Devlin proudly showed him to Alec, who patted the large horse's face.

"So you're gonna win a race, are ya, mate?" he said to the horse.

"Well! What about us?" Saraia's indignant voice behind them made them both turn. She was standing on the doorstep, hands on her hips.

Devlin grinned sheepishly and glanced up at Alec. Alec raised his eyebrows and quietly joked, "Is this the new boss, bro?"

Devlin shook his head and whispered, "Uh-uh, if you think *she's* bossy, wait till you meet Uncle George."

As soon as Devlin walked towards her she melted into a smile and gave him a hug. "I've baked a banana-chocolate cake, can't wait for you to try it. We want to tell you all about our holiday."

"Saraia, this is Alec," Devlin introduced them.

She shook Alec's hand. "Hi, Alec. Thanks for bringing Devlin home. Come in for a coffee and some cake."

They all traipsed into the lounge, where Uncle George was putting the jug on. He came out of the kitchen, hugged Devlin and shook Alec's hand.

"Glad you brought my boy back," George said gruffly to Alec.

"Not a problem, eh," Alec replied. "He's been telling me all about his racehorse."

George nodded. "Yep – that's the next project, eh Saraia?"

She nodded, busy cutting pieces of cake and placing

it on saucers for everybody. "Sure is. I'm looking forward to driving him to his first win. Eat up everybody."

Devlin felt all his uncertainty about the new family arrangements melting away as they talked and George and Saraia laughingly shared some of their honeymoon stories.

His mind drifted to Zak … if given the chance, would he run to win this time?

Next day, everyone was back into their usual Monday routine. The only difference was that Saraia had breakfast cooked and waiting for them when Devlin and George came in from first chores, which meant more time for school. Saraia came into the study and covered some of the subjects with him, using the computer she had brought when she moved in. It made an interesting change from having only George all the time.

"You're gonna have to work extra hard from now on," George warned him. "If I think your racehorse is distracting you from your work, you know which one will be put out to pasture."

Devlin pushed himself harder, making sure to do everything that was asked of him. There was no way he wanted to miss out on seeing his horse race!

After several more weeks of training, George announced it was time for a fast work-out. "We'll take him into Alexandra Park in the morning when there's hardly anybody there and Saraia can see how he goes."

That night Devlin lay in bed feeling too excited to sleep. But the long day soon had its usual effect on him and he fell into a peaceful sleep.

The next morning had an electric air about it, as Devlin and George did the chores. It felt to Devlin as if the horses knew something was up. He had a quick breakfast of cereal and went straight back outside again.

Devlin cleaned Zak's hooves and brushed him down. He replaced his cover and made sure all the gear was in the horse truck. Together, Devlin and George loaded Zak onto the truck and closed the door. They hung the sulky on the outside of the door and tied it on securely. Then all three piled into the front of the cab and George drove carefully down the drive. At last, they were off.

Only a couple of other trainers were at the track working their horses, so there was plenty of space to tie Zak up and put his gear on.

Saraia donned her safety vest, helmet and gloves and climbed into the sulky, ready to drive. George and Devlin followed as she walked the horse quietly onto the track. She walked him the opposite way around the track for a short distance, then turned him back and clicked him into an easy jog.

"You gonna give her instructions?" Devlin asked George.

"She already knows what to do," said George. "She'll warm him up first, then quicken up in stages. At the end she'll let him give all he's got."

"Then we'll know for sure if he's gonna race?"

"Yep. Then we'll know."

Devlin said no more and watched driver and horse like a hawk. Saraia did everything George said she would. Finally, George said, "Here we go!"

He clicked a stopwatch in his hand and timed the last part of the horse's run. Devlin could see Zak was pacing flat out, but he wasn't experienced enough to know if it was fast enough to race. He waited impatiently for George to say something.

George clicked the stopwatch again. "Good."

"What do you mean?" Devlin asked, frustrated.

"He'll race."

"Yee-ha!" Devlin let out a yell of excitement. "When?"

"Soon."

Saraia jogged Zak for a while longer, cooling him off and bringing his heart rate down. When she brought him off the track she was grinning from ear to ear.

"Well, whaddaya know?" she said. "Seems we have ourselves a racehorse."

Devlin suffered impatiently through a two-week wait for Zak's race night. Meanwhile, Saraia arranged a get-together at the local hot pools. Aroha came, as well as Aunty Rose, Uncle Jack, Helena, Zachary and Sammy, Aunty Ange, Uncle Paul, Tracy and Jade, Allan and Jackie. The group had a shared lunch and then spent the afternoon relaxing in the pools.

Devlin had a wonderful time with the kids, splashing and laughing. Saraia and Uncle George enjoyed the younger children too, spending time playing with them and getting to know them better. Saraia spent a lot of time cuddling Jade, giving Aunty Ange the opportunity to relax in the heated pools.

At the end of the afternoon, everyone departed, tired but happy. Devlin guessed the yawning children would fall asleep on their way home. This time his usual sadness at saying goodbye lifted quickly as his excitement about the coming race mounted.

Finally, the night of Zak's race arrived and Devlin's eyes were bright with anticipation. The horse wasn't racing until later in the evening, but the group arrived early at Alexandra Park Raceway so that Saraia was on time for her evening's line-up of drives.

She went off to attend to her duties. George, Allan and Devlin saw to it that Zak was happy and relaxed in his stall, then went into the stands to watch the first race.

Saraia was again driving Smooth Buttercup, horse number three, which was the favourite. Seconds into the start of the race, the announcer interrupted his calling with, "Oh dear! There's been an accident – looks like Jumping Beans and Smooth Buttercup have had a tangle. Smooth Buttercup is down. There's a driver on the track. It looks like ... yes – it's Saraia Selleck. She's up on her feet now, but the ambulance is attending."

Devlin and the men stood, trying to see. "I'd better go!" George exclaimed worriedly and he rushed off down the stairs. Moments later he met up with the ambulance as it came off the track.

Devlin and Allan saw him have brief words with the paramedic then leap into the ambulance to be with Saraia. The ambulance headed off to the hospital.

Allan and Devlin looked at each other, worried and shocked.

"Will she be all right?" Devlin asked, his voice shaky.

"I hope so. It may not be as bad as it looks. Let's go

back to the horse. There's just us here for him now."

Devlin reached Zak first, still standing quietly in his stall. He gave his neck a pat and said quietly, half to himself. "Oh, man – maybe you're not going to race tonight after all."

"Is Saraia going to be all right?" It was Gallion, appearing to look concerned.

Devlin shrugged his shoulders.

"Don't know – I'm certainly praying she will be," Allan replied.

"Want me to drive your horse in the meantime?"

Allan considered for a moment. "Devlin?" he asked.

"I've driven him before, I know the horse," Gallion added persuasively.

"I guess it'll have to be okay, under the circumstances," Devlin conceded. He didn't feel happy about it, but couldn't see a better option.

"Great. I'll see you when it's time to get him out there. You'll be okay gearing up and finding his number and all that?"

Allan nodded. "Yep – done that plenty of times. Colours are here too."

Gallion nodded and went on his way.

"Would Uncle George have put him on Zak?" Devlin asked Allan.

"I'm not sure. He'd have to find somebody, or else scratch the horse from the race. Depends how much you want him to run."

"I want him to run, but what if Zak doesn't like that driver? He's never done any good for him before."

"True. Might not have had anything to do with the driver ... then again, it might."

Allan rubbed his chin thoughtfully. "Anyway, you've made a decision, let's stick with it and hope for the best, eh? Let's just busy ourselves getting this horse ready for his race. You wait here a moment while I go and notify the officials of the driver change."

As soon as he came back, Allan took Zak for a walk to the horse latrine, in case the horse needed to empty his bladder. Devlin walked along with him, then spotted Gallion walking further down the stable area. "Think I'll just have a word with Gallion – race instructions Uncle George gave Saraia."

Allan nodded and carried on. Devlin walked briskly to catch up with Gallion. The driver was also striding out at a fast pace and had reached the horse truck park before Devlin reached him. "Gallion, can I—?"

Gallion turned, startled to see him there. "Look mate, I'll be with ya shortly, okay? Just got something urgent to attend to."

Devlin left his sentence unfinished and nodded. He turned as if to go back to the stables but, suddenly suspicious, as soon as he was out of Gallion's sight he turned to follow him once more, this time secretly. He watched Gallion disappear into the dark between two horse trucks.

Silently he followed and stopped on the other side of the truck nearest him. Bending down and looking underneath, he thought he could see two pairs of legs, one wearing white driver's trousers and the other a black suit. Devlin dropped to the ground and crawled under the truck, so as to hear the conversation.

The stranger was talking quietly. "Good news that that sheila's out of the way. Manage to score any of her drives?"

Gallion replied, whispering. "Yeah – including that horse I used to drive – Brand New Tyre."

"You gonna hook him up again? Help set up the race?"

"Yeah, wouldn't look good if he suddenly won tonight, people might get suspicious of the previous drives, ya know?"

"Right. That's fine, so long as I know. With you driving for my results, it sure increases the chances of picking them, dunnit?"

"Yeah, but I get the feeling … one wrong move, you know? Maybe we should quit for a while, lay low and just enjoy the money."

"What? Chicken out and miss all that money? If you were working for a coward you wouldn't have that flash car of yours, eh. What other drives did you score tonight?"

Devlin heard Gallion mentioning some other horse numbers and races but decided he had heard enough. He didn't understand everything but he'd heard the one thing that concerned *him*. 'Hook 'em up' meant Gallion was not going to drive his horse to win!

Careful not to make any noise, Devlin slipped out from under the truck and went back to the stables, wondering what he should do. *Perhaps Allan will find another driver,* Devlin thought desperately.

There was no sign of Allan at the stall, so he busied himself with putting Zak's gear on. It was important it was done right, something not done up properly could mean disaster.

The night seemed to drag on, with race after race going slowly by. Devlin watched on the television screen provided in the stables, noting that not many of Gallion's drives did very well. Allan still hadn't shown up and Devlin's anxiety increased.

Suddenly his horse's turn came and Gallion was walking towards him. Zak was standing, completely geared up, all ready for his driver to claim him. Devlin's mind worked desperately.

"Looking good!" Gallion said cheerfully.

"Yeah … oh, yeah, that's right …" Devlin said, as if suddenly remembering, "this man in a black suit said he needed to speak with you urgently. He said to ask you to meet him in the horse-truck park at the stalls by the entrance gate."

Gallion's face went a shade paler, then he quickly recovered. "Oh – okay, won't be long."

He increased his pace and headed for the parking area. Devlin followed unobtrusively. When he had visited the track for Zak's fast work, he had used a small toilet, near the entrance gate. It was lockable from the inside and outside. Devlin had a plan.

Gallion stopped outside the stalls where the toilet was and peered into the darkness. Devlin walked silently up behind, holding his breath. Gallion stepped into the doorway of the toilet, saying quietly, "You in here, mate?"

Quickly Devlin took a chance and rushed up behind him. He gave him a great shove, then slammed and bolted the door before Gallion had time to think. "Hey!" he shouted.

Devlin left him to it, rushing back to his horse. His mind was in turmoil. He had so badly wanted his horse to run this race and win.

When he reached Zak, Allan was standing there looking worried. "Where were you? Never mind, you've done a good job gearing up – I've double-checked everything – but where's our driver?"

Before Devlin had a chance to explain, Allan said, "Maybe he's still in the changing room. I'd better tell him to hurry up." Allan rushed off.

Devlin looked desperately at his horse, then at the boxes that held George's racing colours. He noticed that Saraia had left her spare driver's uniform with the colours. "Never hurts to be prepared," he remembered her saying, more than once.

Quickly Devlin crouched down in the stall in front of his horse's nose and changed into the driver's attire. He found his helmet, buckled it on and lastly zipped up the jacket emblazoned with George's racing colours. Taking care not to look directly at anybody, and trying to act as casual and professional as Saraia, he took the reins, unhooked the horse, did up the overcheck and turned him to walk out to the birdcage.

Fortunately, Zak behaved like the true gentleman he was and made it easy for Devlin to look like a professional driver. They got out there just as the bugle call sounded and the clerk of the course was leading the horses onto the track. They slipped neatly into their numbered slot and, at the same time, Devlin quickly climbed into the sulky. His heart was beating crazily as he steered Zak to follow the horse and driver in front of them, onto the brightly lit race track.

CHAPTER FIFTEEN

Meantime, Allan returned to the stall. Seeing the horse gone, he relaxed, assuming Gallion had arrived and taken the horse. He grabbed his race-book and headed up to the stands.

"Hey, mate, grab your rein!" The driver behind Devlin drew his attention to the rein he hadn't sat on properly, allowing the end to drag dangerously on the ground. Hands shaking, Devlin pulled it up and secured it. He didn't dare look around at the man who had spoken to him. He let his helmet sit low over his eyes, hoping no one would realise he wasn't a professional driver.

Please just think I'm a visiting driver, he silently begged.

He did his best to copy the other drivers, warming his horse up around the track, but taking care not to get too close to anybody, or do anything to draw suspicion. Then all too soon, the mobile starting gate was there.

Devlin felt sick with nerves, he could only go by what he had seen the other drivers do from a distance. He walked in circles until it was time to find his number on the gate, then headed towards it. Like a dream horse, Zak walked up to it confidently and locked into position, reminding Devlin that, although *he* was an absolute beginner, his horse wasn't. *I'm trusting you, big boy, to get us through this.*

The mobile began to pick up speed and Devlin was surrounded at close quarters by horses and drivers. The sound of all the pounding hooves sent adrenalin coursing through his veins. He forgot his nerves with the excitement; he was driving his horse – in a race – and he was going to do his best to win!

He was glad now that he had listened so carefully to Uncle George's instructions for Saraia. It hadn't sounded too hard, quite safe really. He was to get a position one out from the rail, with preferably only one horse directly in front of him. This position was nicknamed the 'one-one'. He should stay there as long as he could without getting boxed in, then let his horse out and go for it.

Uncle George had warned Saraia that there were some reasonable horses in this race and not to waste any power if she could help it. Devlin knew he was disadvantaged by his lack of experience compared to the drivers around him. He almost forgot to breathe with the excitement of the moment.

He could feel the hot breath of the horse behind him and suddenly remembered Saraia and her accident. Fear twisted his gut as he realised the possible danger and just how vulnerable he was. He gripped the reins tighter, all senses wildly alert to everything going on around him. Then, suddenly, the mobile gate arms were going up and it was drawing away from him, leaving the horses to battle for the front.

For a moment, Devlin thought he was going to be stuck three wide on the track, but then suddenly the horse on the inside of him broke into a gallop and dropped back, leaving a space for him to slot into. Not believing his luck he realised he was in the position Uncle George had hoped for. He kept his horse close behind the driver in front of him, knowing he shouldn't let Zak drift back, in case a driver on the inside tried to push out.

The horses were all running well, and Devlin managed to hold his position, while the lead driver set the speed of the race. The front group of horses made a complete circuit of the track without changing position. Then Devlin heard the bell signalling the last lap. He kept an ear out for any horse trying to come up outside of him. With 800 metres to go, a horse was coming up from behind. Devlin made his move and pulled Zak's head gently to the left, asking him to come out from behind the horse in front and to change into top gear.

Zak responded fiercely, showing all the heart Devlin knew he had. They passed the two frontrunners quickly and took the lead heading into the straight. Other horses were also coming with him from behind. He could hear shouts and yells from the drivers as they battled to win.

Devlin shouted too. "Yeah! Go boy, go!" He copied what he had seen Saraia and other drivers do, raising the reins and slightly cuffing them on the side of the horse's rump. It was not painful but a clear signal to the horse to give it his all.

Zak went into an all-out top gear that Devlin didn't know he was capable of and stretched away from the other runners. Devlin was alone as he passed the finishing post, the other drivers having to battle it out for second and third.

Zak continued to run for almost a half lap again before Devlin could pull him up to turn him around. Then he realised he would have to salute the judge and take Zak into the winner's circle. He wondered how much longer he could get away with his deception. Well – his horse was a winner, no matter what. He would behave normally and hope for the best.

He heard his horse's number called out as first place, and the Clerk of the Course escorted him to the winner's circle. He saluted the judge and walked Zak in. Allan was standing there, glancing around the crowd, as if looking for someone. *Looking for me,* Devlin guessed. He got out of the sulky and asked Zak to stand. Even with the excitement of the race just minutes behind him, the sweating horse stood obediently. Devlin was relieved, as he had seen many horses find it difficult to stand still so soon after winning their race.

Allan came over to him, about to say something, then stopped short, his mouth hanging open. He turned a shade of pale grey. His jaw went up and down like a goldfish.

Devlin tried to smile and failed miserably. Then the situation got worse, as Uncle George rushed into the winner's circle. "She's going to be fine," he told Allan as he strode forward. "Just a bit bruised. She sent me to see the race – I got here just in time to see him streak past the winning post!" He turned to Devlin. "Well done!

Wh–wh–?"

Like Allan, his mouth fell open in disbelief. Then, at the same time as his face was turning from white, to grey to red and finally purple, he found his tongue. "WHAT?"

"G–Gallion was going to make him lose ..." Devlin tried to explain.

"Photo!" The photographer tried to get their attention, but only Zak stood nicely for the click of the camera.

At that moment four very official-looking men entered. All were wearing smart suits. "Who are you?" the shortest of the men demanded of Devlin. Then he turned to George. "We don't know who your driver is." The short, stocky man turned back to Devlin, looking at him closely. "I don't know you – are you licensed to drive? Are you even *old* enough to *have* a licence?"

Devlin shook his head glumly, his heart sinking quickly from victory to 'uh-oh'.

The man continued sternly. "Then I'm afraid this horse will be disqualified. I want to see you all in the inquiry room immediately!"

Allan finally regained his senses. "Uh, gentlemen, let's just get the horse back to the stables then we'll all come to the inquiry room and get this sorted. I think the explanation is going to take some time."

The men all nodded and departed, looking gravely

serious. "In all my time in racing, I've never heard of anything like it!" one of them muttered as they left the circle.

Devlin took Zak back to the stable and concentrated on ungearing him. George and Allan helped in silence. Devlin heard a siren go, followed by the announcer saying that the winner was disqualified. He swallowed nervously. His moment of elation when he passed the winning post with Zak had been replaced with the sick feeling that he was in more trouble than he had ever been in his whole life.

Zak was stripped of his harness and hosed down. George asked another trainer who had finished racing for the night to walk him and look after him while they went to sort things out.

Devlin felt very subdued as they walked into the inquiry room. The four men eyed him sternly. Devlin decided a school principal's office was nothing compared to this. Then the same man who had spoken to him in the winner's circle introduced himself as the stipendiary steward and began the questioning.

"George, Saraia was supposed to be the driver of your horse. I understand she had an accident, giving you very short notice to appoint another driver."

George nodded. "I went with her in the ambulance.

I didn't have time to appoint another driver at all."

Then Allan cleared his throat. "Uh ... Gallion Bayes approached us and asked to have the drive. We said yes, and I made the change official. When the time came for the horse to race, Gallion was nowhere to be found."

Devlin took a deep breath and spoke up. "Actually ... I overheard Gallion talking to a man in the horse truck area and he said he wasn't going to drive my horse to win. So ... I locked him in the toilet by the entrance gate. I couldn't think what else to do. I saw the driving uniform there and – I guess I just really wanted my horse to race." After he finished speaking he didn't dare look at anyone.

"Young man," the stipendiary steward addressed him sternly, "not driving a horse to win is against the rules. It is totally unacceptable. What motive would Gallion have for it?"

Two of the other men whispered to each other then one of them stood up and quickly left the room.

"I don't know, exactly," Devlin said quietly. "I think it had something to do with the other man, the one in the black suit he was talking to."

The steward placed pen and paper in front of Devlin. "Write down everything you overheard, as accurately as possible."

Devlin picked up the pen and, frowning with

concentration, began to write. Allan removed his notebook from his inside jacket pocket. "I may have some interesting observations to add to Devlin's story. I've been suspicious about race fixing for some time now." He offered his open notebook to the men.

After a few minutes the stipendiary steward said sternly, "If what you have here is true, it will be seriously looked into." He glared at Devlin. "An unlicensed driver in a race is also completely against the rules. Have you even driven at any trial work-outs before?"

Devlin shook his head.

"Do you realise how dangerous and foolish it was for you to attempt driving tonight? You could have been responsible for many horses and drivers getting hurt."

Devlin nodded. "I know. I'm sorry, sir. I acted before I thought it through properly. It's my fault, not Uncle George's or Allan's."

"Even so," the man replied, "this will be discussed further and consequences will follow."

The man who had left the room now returned. He shook his head. "No sign of Gallion now. He smashed his way out of the toilet room. Someone saw him taking off in his car."

The stipendiary steward nodded. "This whole matter needs to be investigated immediately."

Devlin finished writing down his statement of the conversation he'd overheard, including the one he had heard the first time he attended the races. He pushed it towards the men.

The stipendiary steward said curtly, "All right, gentlemen. Thank you – you may go." Devlin stood and followed Allan and George out the door.

The ride home in the truck was stiff and silent at first, as each mulled over what had happened. Tiring of it, Devlin asked, "How is Saraia?"

George stared straight ahead at the road. "She's going to be okay – helmet saved her. She got a bump on the head – saw stars a bit at first – and a few bruises. They're just keeping her in overnight for observation. I'll get her in the morning."

Devlin stole a glance at Allan, wondering what both men were thinking about him and his foolish act. He felt miserable and longed to put his arms around Zak to draw comfort from the big, non-judgmental friend. He stared at the floor.

"So – um, what should the punishment be for him then, George?" Allan spoke finally.

Devlin was surprised to hear a note of amusement in Allan's tone. He looked up and saw the hint of a smile twitching the corners of Allan's otherwise serious mouth.

George shook his head, expressing disbelief. "What would you do with him?" he asked.

Allan couldn't hold it in any longer, he began to laugh. "My goodness!" he chortled. "Of all the things in the world to do!"

George added, "I've never been so embarrassed in my life," but he was beginning to chuckle as well.

"It's going to get worse when it all hits the papers tomorrow," Allan pointed out, holding his side and wiping his face free of laughing tears.

Devlin looked from one man to the other. It was his turn to be speechless. He had been wondering if Uncle George was going to break his 'smack-free' rule and tan his hide, or send him back to Aunty Rose. He certainly hadn't expected this.

George pierced him with a glare, despite his choked up laughter. "Don't you think for a minute that, because we're laughing, what you did was okay, you hear?"

Devlin nodded, feeling sombre inside but a smile beginning to turn up the corners of his mouth. "It was a pretty dumb thing to do," he said. "Zak got disqualified anyway."

"The winner's circle photo will be a classic ..." Allan

said, still trying to control his mirth, "us with our mouths wide open."

"The horse was the only one posing for the camera," Devlin agreed, smiling sheepishly. "At least there was one good thing that came out of it," he added. "Zak won fair and square."

The men broke into fits of chuckling and coughing the rest of the way home.

Allan turned out to be right about the newspapers. Devlin saw headlines over the next few days reading 'Unlicensed Driver Wins and Loses' and 'Scandal Revealed'. The latter article told how an illegal 'setting up' of race results had been exposed and that more facts were coming to light. An unnamed driver was a strong suspect. There was a picture of Zak winning his race with Devlin leaning forward in the sulky. Devlin clipped it out and pinned it to his wall.

As soon as Saraia arrived home, she sat Devlin down and made him tell her the whole story from beginning to end. She scolded him for his recklessness.

After a couple of weeks, the drama began to settle down, though George was still waiting to hear how the officials would discipline Devlin's rule violations. Devlin noticed George and Saraia having secret little talks now and then and wondered what it could be about.

Then, one evening, he answered a knock at the front door. He stood staring at a man who looked like an older version of his own mirror image. "Devlin." The man's voice was deep and confident. "Couldn't be mistaken, could I? It's like looking at a photo of myself. I'm your dad."

Devlin went cold with shock. George and Saraia had come up behind in time to hear the man's statement. They, too, looked stunned.

Saraia found her voice. "Uh, come in, Mr–?"

"Brown, Terry Brown, thanks." He walked into the living room and took an offered seat.

"I know this must be a shock," he said. "There were write-ups of Devlin's horse race in lots of newspapers, including the Australian racing pages. A friend drew my attention to one of Devlin's photos. The resemblance was uncanny. I flew over and searched you all out through some racing contacts." He looked at Devlin. "So you own a good racehorse? He must be worth a bit. I thought maybe you could sell him and come and live with me in Australia."

Devlin sat on the couch, speechless. He finally found his voice. "I – I don't even know you."

"Yes, I understand that. Your mother broke up with me when she was pregnant with you. I was a bit of a jerk in those days. She wouldn't let me know where she was and then I lost contact with her all together. I tried to track her down, but in the end just had to move on. Then I went to Australia. How come you're not living with her?"

Devlin watched the man who was his father, feeling numb and empty. He couldn't trust himself to answer without breaking down in tears. Instead he said, "I've got brothers and sisters – I couldn't leave them."

"They don't live here with you, do they? Are they with your mum?" Terry asked. "If you come to live with me, I've got a big room for you. You can meet my wife, your two stepbrothers and a half-sister. You could come back and visit your other family every now and then."

Devlin felt too overwhelmed to say anymore. He just sat, staring at this stranger who seemed to think he could just walk into his life and claim him back as his son. He didn't know what to feel ... or how he *should* feel.

George spoke up. "I think it's been a big thing for Devlin to meet you today, Terry. It would be fairest to him to give him some time to think about what you've said."

"And to adjust to having a father finally on the scene," Saraia added.

Terry Brown nodded in agreement. "Fair enough. I'm staying in West Auckland for a week, then I'll be flying back. It's Tuesday today – so I'd like an answer by the weekend, if possible."

Devlin nodded. He stood to see his father to the door. They shook hands and the man left. Exhausted, Devlin excused himself and went to his bed. Despite his tiredness, sleep came slowly, as he tossed and turned for a long time.

The next day he woke and wondered if it had all been a dream. He got up and attended the cow as usual. George was wandering around doing the usual morning chores.

"You okay?" George asked.

Devlin nodded. "Was that for real?"

George frowned. "I'm afraid it was. Came as an awful shock to Saraia and me. I can't imagine how you must have felt. I rang Aroha – it was a shock to her too."

"What am I going to do?" Devlin got ready to carry the milk pail inside.

"Well, you have to think about what *you* really want. He's offering you a life with him and to be part of a family."

"But I already have family – and you and Saraia are my family too, now. It's too late for him just to charge in here and think he can suddenly be my family, isn't it? I mean ... I wouldn't mind getting to know him – slowly." He sighed, exasperated. "I don't know where I belong." He took a deep gulp of air as he got ready to ask a question that made him feel vulnerable. "You still want me, don't you?"

"Of course," George replied gruffly. "I've been discussing with Saraia something else as well. But I don't want to tell you until you've thought your Dad's offer through carefully. You let me know, okay?"

Devlin nodded.

After a couple of days, his mind and heart still in turmoil, he turned to Zak for comfort. They went for a quiet ride down to the lake, where Devlin dismounted. He held the end of Zak's lead, letting him graze the sweet grass.

Devlin poured out his heart. "I don't want to sell you, big boy," he told him. "I don't want to go to Australia, either. Not to live, anyway. Maybe for a visit, you know? If my father will let me."

Images of Zachary, Sammy, Tracy and Jade filled his mind. "They need me, you know? The kids. I couldn't just leave them – not now." Sudden peace filled his heart as he pictured their faces and he knew he wouldn't, *couldn't* take up his father's offer.

He grinned at Zak, patting his strong neck. "No, mate – we're going to win some more races – the proper way. I'm going to keep learning how to farm and, as soon as I can, I'm going to reach my goal. I'll have my own place for the kids to come to. Staying here seems safest for now.

Uncle George and Saraia say they still want me."

Feeling a bit better, Devlin mounted Zak and headed back to tell Uncle George and Saraia his decision.

The couple sat on the couch and listened as Devlin told them he wanted to stay.

Saraia looked excited. "You're sure?"

Devlin nodded emphatically. "Yep."

"That's great!" she exclaimed, then added, "Although I don't know how well your dad's going to accept it." Then she looked at George. "Can we tell him?"

George nodded. "Devlin," he began, "we've been doing some serious thinking of our own."

"We've been talking about extending our family," Saraia added.

"Are you going to have a baby?" Devlin asked.

She shook her head. "No."

Devlin looked puzzled.

George spoke again. "It may take some time . . . but we happen to know of four children who might one day like to live with us."

"Four?" Devlin said, perplexed. "Who?"

"In order of age," said George, "Tracy, Zachary, Sammy and Jade."

Devlin's face lit up in a mix of disbelief and elation. "True? They're going to come and live with us, all of them?" He felt stunned as thoughts of this new possibility rushed through his mind.

"Hang on a minute, we don't know yet," Saraia explained. "We need to start by having them over for visits so we can get to know one another. It's important to be sure it'll work before we make any commitments. But we'd like to give it a go and see."

Devlin leaped off the couch and punched the sky in victory. "Ye-ah! Awesome, man! That would be so cool!"

He sat back down and stared at George and Saraia, suddenly overwhelmed by their obvious commitment to him. Saraia came over and gave him a hug. Devlin looked beyond her shoulder at George and caught a glimpse of love shining in the man's sharp blue eyes. Then George came and wrapped them both in a giant bear hug. As the hard, strong arms enveloped him and Saraia, Devlin felt a strong awareness of the whole farm around him and a feeling of safety. His heart gave up some of its insecurities, as he made a decision: *Whatever challenges are to come, this is where I belong.*